Christmas at Moo

Angela Britnell

Choc Lit

Where heroes are like chocolate – irresistible!

www.choc-lit.com

Published 2020 by Choc Lit Limited
Penrose House, Crawley Drive, Camberley, Surrey GU15 2AB, UK
www.choc-lit.com

EPUB: 978-1-78189-464-4
PRINT: 978-1-78189-364-7

Acknowledgements

The Dickens of a Christmas Festival is a long standing tradition in this part of Tennessee, and for over thirty years my wonderful friend John Fraser has immersed himself in the character of Fagin every December and trained generations of 'pickpockets' including my own sons! Without him it simply wouldn't be the same. Thank you to him for helping inspire parts of *Christmas at Moonshine Hollow*.

This book truly came to life when Lee Kennedy, owner of the Leiper's Fork Distillery near my home in Tennessee and his one-of-a-kind tour guide Matt 'Pops' Mayo generously shared their huge enthusiasm and knowledge with me. Thanks also to them.

As ever, thanks must also go to the Tasting Panel readers who said 'yes' to the manuscript and made publication possible: Alma Hough, Anne Eckersley, Carol Dutton, Deborah Warren, Sharon Walsh, Monica Mac, Donna Morgan, Fran Stevens, Haley Eyre and Honor Gilbert.

Chapter One

'Would it kill you to try smiling today, Cole?' Exasperation oozed out of his mother as she corralled him in his office.

She'd caught him in the middle of slipping on one of the smart, dark green official Landon Hollow Distillery collared shirts. Another strike against him. If his mother had her way he'd wear them day in and day out for work, instead of whatever ratty old T-shirt he grabbed first in the morning.

'I know you dislike taking the tours around, but people like to see the face behind the name.' Her blue eyes sparkled. 'Even if it is a miserable one.'

Cole briefly considered protesting that his great-grandfather, the notorious moonshiner 'Lightning' Landon, would laugh at the idea of conducting tours to show off the handmade copper still he used to make his illegal moonshine. It'd been hidden deep in the nearby woods in an area that old-time local people still affectionately called Moonshine Hollow. He swiftly abandoned the idea as asking for more trouble.

'Sorry, Mother.' He pulled the edges of his mouth into a fake smile. 'Is that better?'

'Not much, but it'll have to do.' Sylvia tugged at one of the shaggy, dark blond curls hanging down under his baseball cap. 'Any chance you can fit a haircut into your busy social life this week?'

Another dig. They both knew he basically lived in the distillery. Ever since he'd chucked in his job as a corporate lawyer in Washington DC a decade ago and returned to Tennessee, he'd changed from one sort of workaholic to another.

Cole made a point of checking his watch. 'If you've finished hasslin' me, I've got a dozen people waiting to hear all about the one hundred year history of Landon moonshine.' He watched her face tighten. Sylvia fought a constant inner battle between enjoying the proceeds of the business and accepting that her late husband's grandfather spent most of his adult life as a wanted man. 'Is it okay if I pop over for dinner tonight?' Her stern expression softened. Spending an evening listening to his pompous stepfather wasn't

Cole's idea of a good time, but it wouldn't kill him to make the occasional effort.

'Of course. Betty's fixing a pot roast.' Her nose wrinkled. 'You know we mostly stick to fish and chicken for the sake of our health, but Martin complained yesterday that he hadn't seen a piece of red meat in months.'

'Awesome. I picked the right night. Nobody makes pot roast like Miss Betty.'

'You men are all the same.' The indulgent tone indicated he'd been forgiven.

'I'll walk out with you.' He suddenly wondered why she'd come in the first place. 'Was there something you needed, Mother? We don't often see you here.' Cole opened the door for her.

'I've been having a wander around to get some more ideas for the distillery's Christmas decorations. We'll need to put them up next week after Thanksgiving.'

'Oh right. Thanks.' He'd prefer the distillery not to be decked out in tinsel and baubles but held his tongue. After his father died the year Cole turned thirteen, he'd lost his appetite for celebrating Christmas and had never really got it back.

'Don't worry. It will be tasteful and appropriate.'

Two words that nailed his mother to a T.

'There was something else … but it can wait.' An added flush tinged her cheeks. 'We'll talk later.'

There was no point in pressing. She wouldn't explain until she was good and ready. That was a gene they definitely shared.

The black hoodie covered Jenna's distinctive red hair but didn't look out of place on a cold November morning. She inched around to the back of the small group of people gathered around the rough-carved oak bar where they had been asked to wait for their guide.

'Hi y'all, and welcome to Landon Hollow Distillery. I'm Cole Landon the fourth, great grandson of "Lightning" Landon.'

Everyone paid attention to the man, but he was the sort of man people would always notice – tour guide or not. His physical appearance was arresting enough; most women would find his tall, broad-shouldered figure easy on the eyes, but it was his air of suppressed energy that couldn't be ignored. It was corralled now into doing a task he had little appetite for, judging by the barely-there smile that kept a safe distance from his dark eyes.

The jolt of his deep, drawling voice made her eyes prickle. The rich, honeyed tones reminded Jenna of her favourite grandfather, because Jimmy Richards never lost his Southern accent despite living in England for over sixty years until his recent death. Cole launched into the history of his family's involvement in illegal moonshine and she was disappointed, but not surprised, when there was no mention of her great grandfather, 'Tucker' Richards.

Her heart thudded when he began to ask everyone where they'd come from. She'd avoided speaking to anyone else yet, but her accent would be impossible to disguise in this sea of Americans.

'How about you, ma'am?'

As their gazes locked, Jenna's face heated up. 'Uh, I'm from England.'

'What brought you to our neck of the woods?'

Everyone stared as though she had two heads.

'I'm on holiday.'

'Great. We don't get many visitors this time of year. Right everyone, let's get goin'. I know y'all want to see how we make our products and then get around to the good part. The tastings. We've developed several new flavours for the holiday season I think you're gonna love.'

A distinctive warm, yeasty scent wafted out as he pushed open a set of heavy wood doors, and she trailed after the rest of the group into the distillery. They stopped in front of a massive copper still, its chimney soaring all the way to the top of the high roof.

'Moonshine is basically unaged whisky so the distillation processes are very similar. The main difference is that we bottle our product almost immediately instead of ageing it in barrels. I'll run through the process quickly, then I'm happy to go into as much or as little detail as y'all are interested in hearing.'

Before coming here she'd done her research and, although chemistry was never her strong suit, she understood that the basic recipe he was explaining now revolved around the fact that yeast plus sugar equalled ethanol.

'You might not realise that the most crucial ingredient is good water, and the four best places for that are said to be Scotland, Ireland, Kentucky and here in Tennessee. We're fortunate to have our own well and that superb water is the basis of everything we make.'

Jenna couldn't help being drawn in as Cole showed them samples of the grains they used – corn, wheat and rye that were all farmed locally and milled there in the distillery.

'Almost seven hundred gallons of water goes in this mash tank every morning and that's heated up before the grain is added and stirred to do its magic. Once the alcohol is excreted the spent mash goes back to a local farmer to feed his cows.' Cole pointed to another massive tank. 'That's where the fermentation happens. It takes a few days for the sugar to convert to ethanol. Then it's the turn of "Bubbling Bertha" to do her magic.' He lovingly stroked the burnished copper as if it was a beautiful woman. 'We're particularly proud of her because she's an almost exact replica of the one my great grandfather made with his own hands and used in the woods outside this building. We had to make a few modifications and build it on a larger scale to cope with an increase in volume, but I like to think he would be proud.'

His smile was less forced now and the deep lines etched around his mouth had smoothed out. She guessed they must be around same age but, if they were, he wore his thirty-eight years much heavier. At least she liked to think so, although her mirror might disagree on some days.

'The vapour rises into the condenser and turns back into liquid and that's the first run over. The second run produces three stages known as heads, hearts and tails but only the hearts are bottled. The heads are full of waste products.' He grinned. 'Drink that and you're likely to live up to the old sayin' about being blind running drunk. The tails aren't as lethal but they're still unpleasant, although a certain amount can be saved to redistill later.' Cole looked thoughtful. 'The art of knowing how to recognise those three stages is the basis of the distiller's craft. I studied a lot before I started to make moonshine, but the knack of knowin' when to cut off distillation comes with practise. I had the best teacher goin'.' He pointed to a grey-haired man in bib overalls across the distillery. 'That's Tommy. He's forgotten more about moonshine distilling than I'll probably ever know.'

The tour continued over to the bottling section, and it was clear that Cole had a good rapport with his workers. He didn't strike her as a man burdened with guilt over the distillery's success but perhaps he didn't know the full story? If her Grandpa Jimmy was right then 'Lightning' Landon and his descendants had done her family a great disservice. Cole Landon was the living, breathing embodiment of that legacy, and she must never forget it.

Chapter Two

Cole answered Bubba Wilson, a visitor from Kentucky, while keeping an eye on the English woman hovering on the far edge of the group. He swapped light-hearted banter with the jovial man who was putting down moonshine in comparison to traditional Kentucky bourbon.

'Come and taste some. That'll convert you.'

'About time. A man could die of thirst waitin' for a drink around here.' Bubba gave Cole's arm a good-natured jab.

He got everyone's attention. 'If no one has any further questions, we'll head off to the tasting room.'

'I do have one actually.' The British woman's clipped tones took him aback. 'You mentioned your great grandfather's recipe, so is that something he created himself?'

'Yeah, he sure did. When we're in the retail store you'll see his handwritten recipe framed on the wall. There's also a whole timeline on display showing the heritage of the Landon Hollow Distillery.'

She pushed her hood back slightly and the bright lights enabled him to see her face properly. The searing Tennessee summer heat wouldn't be kind to that clear, porcelain skin, and he idly wondered how quickly it would reveal a blush. On cue, a soft, rosy glow spread up from her neck and bloomed on her cheeks. Cole wasn't aware that he'd been staring. He strode off and beckoned for them all to follow him. Thankfully, his cousin Debbie was at the tasting bar ready to take over. She was his polar opposite and the quintessential people person. They shared the tour duties, but the difference was she actually enjoyed it.

'We've got some of our old favourites for you to try, including the original Lightning Flash, but this year we're also experimenting with some seasonal specials.' Cole picked up a bottle with red flames on the label. 'This one is Cinnamon Fire.' He twitched a grin. 'It lives up to its name, so watch out if you're a moonshine novice. For a gentler introduction, I'd recommend you try Ambrosia Angel.' Cole showed off the opaque white bottle. 'If you're familiar with the traditional southern dessert, you'll appreciate the coconut and pineapple notes.' He lifted another bottle with a festive green and red label. 'Mistletoe Madness is my number one choice, although I'm not promisin' it'll get you kissed.' That elicited a round of laughter. 'I think the spice and smoke layers set it apart, but I'll be interested to hear what y'all like best.' He could wax lyrical for hours about his creations but reined himself in. When his last girlfriend, Lori, dumped him she complained that it was worse than dating a chemist. 'Debbie will pour the drinks and I'll hang around to answer any questions.' Cole stepped to one side and wiped his damp hands on his jeans, thankful that was the last tour for the week. Nobody nabbed him straight away, so he ambled off to one side where he could observe them all. There were a few surprised expressions when people tasted their samples; most of the reactions were pleasant, but there were a few wrinkled noses. He watched Mary Poppins; the name he'd given to their mystery Brit. She had the same crystal-clear voice as her namesake but, like the fictional character, he suspected there was more to her.

Most of his guests were laughing while they drank and having a good time but not Miss Poppins. Her frown deepened and it struck him she was mentally taking notes. When they first began doing tours last year, one of his fellow distillers warned him about possible spies.

'*Keep your eyes open, Cole. There are a lot of new folks in this game and they aren't all honourable. I make it clear in my introduction that they aren't to take pictures of the equipment. When I caught one man and challenged him, he admitted he was from one of the Knoxville outfits.*'

It was time to do some tactful digging. Cole grabbed a bottle of Snickerdoodle Star off the shelf and a couple of tasting glasses. He plastered on something resembling a warm smile and inched around to his quarry.

Even over the swirl of aromas filling the air, she caught his scent. Clean, fresh soap. Air-dried clothes. Why were those particular scents so distinctive and appealing?

'Mr Cole, thank you for the tour.' Jenna swung around to face him. 'It was most informative.'

'Glad to hear it.' He sounded awkward. 'How about joining me in a shot of this little beauty?'

Was he making a pass at her? Normally she wouldn't object, but a voice in her head said to watch out. 'Why not?' Jenna tilted her head to read the label. 'If it's any good, I'll have to buy a bottle for my mother. Snickerdoodles are her absolute favourite biscuits.' Cole's eyes narrowed. She realised now they were an unusual shade of silver-grey. In the distance they'd appeared much darker because of his long, soot-black lashes.

'Y'all have them in the UK?'

'No, but her father was American. She's never lived here, though.'

'What part of the States were they from?'

'Oh, actually, around here somewhere, but I don't know much more than that because they lost contact years ago. I might check on it while I'm here.' The half-truth would suffice for now.

'Are you hanging around this area long?'

'I'm not sure yet.'

'I guess you'll be goin' back before the holidays?'

'Probably.' She took the tiny glass he offered and quickly took a sip to avoid going into any more detail about why she was there. 'Oh, wow. That's absolutely delicious. I thought it would be too sweet, but it's not. How did you manage that?'

'That would be telling.'

She sensed him pull away.

'You'll have to excuse me. I need to talk with some of the other folk. Enjoy the rest of your time in Tennessee, Ms … you didn't tell me your name?'

'Jenna Pendean.'

Cole slipped off his cap and ran his hand over his messy blond curls before tugging the hat back on again. She suspected that was a nervous habit and wondered if it was down to her. He gave a curt nod and strode off.

The bubbly young woman had finished serving the drinks and moved to the retail side of the room where she'd joined another older woman who was busy behind the cash register. Jenna really needed to get her alone to pump her for more information but would have to bide her time. She noticed one of the other visitors taking pictures and decided to follow suit. The timeline painted around the walls would make an interesting addition to her research so she'd start with that. Next, she lingered in front of the supposedly original recipe for Lightning Flash.

As a child, Jenna had spent endless happy hours listening to her Grandpa Jimmy's stories when her parents were busy at work in their family pub. He'd moved down to Cornwall from Somerset to live with them in The Green Parrot after her grandmother died. When her mother warned her that Grandpa Jimmy's stories were all nonsense she stopped repeating them, but they remained stuck in her head. After her grandfather's death she helped her mum sort through his things and they discovered a battered cardboard box full of assorted mementos and papers. Jenna offered to sort through them and came across an old yellowing letter Grandpa Jimmy had shown to her years earlier. She clearly recalled what he'd said at the time.

'If old "Lightning" Landon's people ever get to making moonshine again this is our claim to half the profits, but the money isn't what's important, Jenna. My old father "Tucker"

Richards helped to make the recipe for Lightning Flash, and he's entitled to a fair share of the credit.'

Jenna had spent hours deciphering the letter, but when she explained to her mother what it said Anne had laughed, telling her it was nothing but a worthless agreement between two old drunks. Of course Jenna couldn't let it go, and when she poked around online for information on a Landon family in Tennessee, the distillery website popped up. Now she was here to discover the truth.

The crowd was thinning, so she selected a couple of bottles and headed for the cash register. 'Hello. It's Debbie, isn't it?'

'Yeah.' A wide grin lit up the young woman's pretty, heart-shaped face. 'You're English.'

'I certainly am.' Then she shamelessly made the most of her curiosity and discovered that Debbie was Cole's cousin. The youngest of five children, she was the only one still living at home with her parents and grandmother a few minutes back down the road from the distillery.

'Where are you staying? In Nashville?'

'Uh, here in Leiper's Fork. I've rented an adorable cottage for a fortnight.'

'Are you a country music fan?' Debbie asked.

'Not really, although I haven't ever heard much so that could be unfair.'

'Have you been to Puckett's or heard of it?'

'No, I only arrived a couple of days ago. What is it?' Jenna queried.

'It's a cute little restaurant and shop that's been in the centre of Leiper's Fork forever. There's an open mic night this evening at six and I'm goin' with a few of my girlfriends. It could be awful or you might hear someone awesome. Do you fancy comin' along?'

'I'd love to.' *Would it hurt to be a normal tourist for a few hours?*

‘We could meet early and have a wander around the few stores first. You might pick up some Christmas presents.’

She had half-promised to spend Christmas with her mother in Watford this year which would irk her father, but ever since her parents split up it was a balancing act to keep them both happy. A flare of rebellion snaked through her. ‘I might end up staying here for the holidays. I haven’t decided yet.’

‘Oh, right.’ Debbie looked puzzled.

‘What time do you want to get together later?’ She noticed Cole giving her another penetrating stare from across the room.

‘Five? We’ll meet you there.’

‘Great.’ Jenna paid then grabbed the distinctive green and gold bag from Debbie and strolled back out into the pale winter sunshine. She took a few calming breaths before heading for her rental car. Why had she ever thought she was cut out for this sort of subterfuge?

Chapter Three

Cole considered taking the scissors to his freshly washed hair but abandoned that as a lousy idea. His mother would have a fit if he wore his baseball cap at the dinner table, so she'd have to tolerate his shaggy mop instead. He grabbed his wallet and keys and ran his fingers wistfully over the biography of Thomas Jefferson he was reading. It sat on top of a pile of books lying on the table by his battered old leather recliner. A fire was already laid in the stone fireplace and only needed a match to flicker into life. If he fixed a frozen pizza and grabbed a couple of beers, he'd have the makings of a damn near perfect evening. Cole sighed and headed outside to his truck.

As they'd done too many times already, Jenna Pendean's sapphire-blue eyes, clear pale skin and air of mystery sneaked back into his brain. He would love to believe the distillery's fame had spread far enough to lure in international visitors, but that was unlikely. November was hardly prime tourist season either. Debbie was cagey earlier when he nabbed her and tried a little subtle interrogation to discover what she and Jenna discussed.

'This and that. Why?' Naturally his cousin teased him about having a crush on the English woman. 'I'll put in a good word for you tonight.'

After she explained about Puckett's, he considered warning her not to discuss distillery business, but she would have laughed and called him a boring old so and so.

The roads were relatively quiet, and about twenty-five minutes later he reluctantly turned into his mother's sweeping driveway. When she remarried, Sylvia insisted that her new husband moved into their family home until Cole graduated from high school. The idea was to give him stability, but every day he was forced to face the reality of another man taking his beloved father's place. Literally. At the head of the table and in his mother's bed.

He swept his gaze over the ostentatious pillared façade of the sprawling Colonial-style house that Martin Buchanan had proudly bought here in Belle Meade, the most exclusive part of Brentwood, the very week after Cole left for college. Four wide semi-circular steps led up to the ornate oak front door and, for the fall season, they were flanked with white pumpkins; eerie looking things in his opinion, but clearly orange ones were too ordinary. A large wreath his mom had created from vibrant fall flowers set off with a massive black velvet bow completed the theme. Cole picked up the gleaming brass pineapple-shaped door knocker and let it drop.

'Come in, my boy.' Martin greeted him and they exchanged fake smiles and firm handshakes. 'Your mother will be down in a minute. You know what the ladies are like.' He steered Cole towards the living room while keeping up a monologue about the stock market. 'Whisky? Or is that too fancy for your palette after that backwoods stuff you churn out?'

Cole accepted the offer and remained tight-lipped. His stepfather was far from the only person to look down on moonshine. The bad reputation lingered from the days when it was made in illegal, homemade stills and often poisoned its customers. The first sip of Martin's whisky told him this had been produced to show off. Single malt. Scottish. Probably upwards of a thousand dollars a bottle.

'There you are, my dear. Beautiful as always.' Martin beamed at his wife.

'Betty says that dinner is ready. Let's go in.'

His stepfather looked wrong-footed at being ignored. Cole's appetite kicked in as they followed the wonderful aromas into the dining room; an extensive rectangular space weighed down with a glittering chandelier and ponderous mahogany furniture.

'That smells incredible, Miss Betty,' he said. The promise to keep on their old housekeeper was another of his mother's non-negotiables when she remarried. 'You're a wonder.'

'And you're still a naughty boy.' She smacked Cole's hand away when he tried to snatch a slice of beef off the platter she was trying to set down. 'We don't see you enough these days.'

'Sorry. I don't have much free time.'

Betty gave him an arch look as though he should make more time for what was important.

'Sit down and eat before it gets cold.'

They all did as they were told, and Cole took care not to buck the rules of polite dinner conversation while they ate.

'Would you care to join me in my study for another taste of that fine whisky?' Martin offered as soon as they were through. If he declined that would seem rude, but he had no desire for another 'bonding' session.

'There's something I need to speak with Cole about.' Sylvia tapped her manicured nails against her wine glass. She pushed away her plate, and he noticed the food was virtually untouched. His mother watched what she ate very carefully but always made an exception for pot roast, so he wondered what was up. 'Alone.'

A wariness crept into Martin's watery, blue eyes.

'Come with me,' Sylvia snapped. 'I'll ask Betty to delay bringing in the coffee for a while.'

He followed her into the living room but as soon as she closed the living room door behind them, his mother burst into tears.

'Oh, Cole I've been a fool. I trusted Martin and he's lost everything we have.' Sylvia kept her voice low and gave a helpless wave around the room. 'He's liquidated all our investments over the last few years to pay off debts, but it wasn't enough.' Her eyes flooded with pain. 'We'll have to sell the house. My shares in the distillery are gone too. Martin sold them to pay back more creditors.'

Cole's mind spun and he thought he might throw up. When he'd first started the distillery, his mother had invested a chunk of the money she'd inherited on his father's death so they were fifty-fifty partners in Landon Hollow. He swallowed before he asked the question he was afraid to know the answer to. 'Who owns half of my business now?'

Jenna tightened the belt on her cherry-red wool coat. Once the sun went down, the air carried a sharp reminder that it was late November. Cute wasn't a word in her normal vocabulary, but Debbie hadn't exaggerated when she used that label for Leiper's Fork. It was only about a five-minute wander from her rental cottage down to the main street. She could imagine the shops on a postcard – several were situated in log cabins and every one was unique. From the outside it was obvious that most blurred the line between Thanksgiving and Christmas when it came to decorations – there was an abundance of pumpkins and corn sheaves among the fairy lights and plastic snowmen.

'We're over here!' Debbie waved frantically from the front porch of a small art gallery. 'Come meet the girls.'

She could blame the lingering remnants of jet-lag but suspected that even wide awake and alert, she would have struggled to keep up with her new friend's rambling introductions. Debbie's appealing Southern drawl didn't help matters. As far as she could make out Jess, blonde and petite, was a high school maths teacher. Mandy, a curvy brunette, worked in a spa and tall, skinny Vicky worked in banking.

'It's great to meet you all, and thank you for inviting me to join you.'

'OMG, you sound like Lady Mary in Downton Abbey.' Mandy giggled. 'Say something else.'

'Don't embarrass the poor thing.' Vicky stepped in to rescue her. 'We've got about half an hour free to raid the stores. I got us a reservation at Puckett's and the show starts at six.'

'It's a good thing this one keeps us organised.' Debbie's smile was good-natured. 'None of us would've graduated high school if she hadn't forced us to study.'

'Don't put yourself down. Cole couldn't manage that place without you. Most of the time he's so miserable he puts the customers off.'

'We can't all be perky,' Jess chimed in. 'Cole's a good guy. Losing his dad that way changes a person.'

'We're wasting valuable shopping time,' Debbie declared, clearly trying to change the subject. 'I vote we head straight for Serenite Maison and Moo Country.' She explained that those particular two shops were their favourites. 'We'll save the rest for another day.'

Somehow, half an hour later, Jenna found herself the proud owner of a pair of scarlet leather cowboy boots tooled in gold from Moo Country that the girls swore she needed. She could have spent far longer in Serenite Maison, with its eclectic mixture of antiques and local crafts, and considered the three fat scented candles she'd bought a modest haul.

'Come on, I'm starving. I've been too busy to eat all day,' Mandy complained.

'Is the menu good?' Jenna asked.

'Oh yeah. It's regular Southern food. Nothing fancy, but if you leave hungry it's your own fault.' Debbie linked arms with her as they crossed the road. 'Puckett's has been here since the 1950s. My folks hung out here when they were datin'.'

The unpretentious building with its red roof and matching red awning was throbbing with life, and music drifted out from the door that was constantly opening and closing with people popping in and out.

'Here's our table.' Vicky led the way. 'I'll go ahead and order the fried pickles and fried green beans while we decide what else we're having.' She noticed Jenna looking bewildered and laughed. 'Sounds weird, I know, but try them and you'll be addicted too. Beer?'

'Uh, yes that would be fine. Something local maybe?'

'Yazoo,' Jess declared. 'I'll have the same.'

They had a prime seat close to the small stage, and for the first time in days Jenna relaxed. She joined in the conversation when she felt like it and let them all chatter away when she didn't. The crowd encouraged the first singer who was a nervous young boy, and three other performers followed before there was a break. Jenna discovered she loved some country music, but not all of it. Rather like the fried pickles. She wouldn't hurry back for a seconds of those, but the fried green beans struck her as an excellent way to disguise one of her least favourite vegetables. All of a sudden the waitress set a mammoth plate of food down in front of her.

'Goodness. Do I eat it or climb it?' Her obvious shock at the size of the Puckett's Famous Burger made the rest of the group laugh. She considered asking for a knife and fork but watched Jess squash hers slightly before picking it up in both hands to take a monster bite, so she followed suit.

'Don't put it down again yet or it'll fall apart,' Jess warned. 'Wait until you're at least half way through.'

There wasn't much conversation while they all got busy eating, but a tiny squiggle of guilt sneaked in when she evaded Mandy's questions about why she'd been drawn to visit this part of Tennessee.

'Hey, girls. How are y'all doin'?' Cole's voice suddenly boomed out from the doorway. He stumbled across the room and dragged a spare chair from another table to flop down between her and Debbie. 'Havin' a good time?' He draped a leaden arm over her shoulder, and she caught a whiff of Cinnamon Fire moonshine on his warm breath.

'Uh yes, thanks.'

Debbie rolled her eyes behind Cole's back and mouthed that they needed to get him out of there.

'I'm still getting over jet-lag, so I'm thinking of calling it a night. Do you want to walk out with me?'

'I'd like to do a whole lot more than that, sweetheart.' His deep drawl turned raspy. 'This is real pretty.' Cole tugged at her loose hair. 'I've always had a weakness for redheads.'

'For heaven's sake, what is goin' on with you?' Debbie gave him a poke in the ribs. 'Sorry, he's not normally like this,' she whispered to Jenna. 'In fact, make that never. If we can get him out to my car, I'll drive him home to my place. It's not far and my folks will take care of him.'

'Of course.'

The other girls offered to help too, but Jenna insisted she was happy to make a move. Somehow they managed to drag him out of there and wedged Cole into the back seat of Debbie's car. He stretched out his long legs and rested his head against the window.

'I sure am sorry about this.' Debbie's cheeks were pink.

'Don't worry. We all overdo it sometimes.'

'Not my cousin.' Her insistence struck Jenna as truthful. 'I'll call you tomorrow, okay? And thanks again.'

'Are you okay to drive?'

'Yeah, I've been drinking iced tea all night. What about you? I could drop you off wherever you're staying.'

'There's no need. My cottage is only a few minutes' walk from here. You take care of Cole and I'll be fine.' Jenna waved goodbye and strolled away up the road. Tomorrow had the potential to be very interesting indeed.

Chapter Four

Cole gripped the bouquet of bronze chrysanthemums and rapped on the door. He had purposely left this apology until last.

'Oh, good morning.' Jenna's lush pink lips curved into a broad smile. 'Or perhaps you don't think so?'

'Not really. These are for you.' He shoved the flowers at her. 'To apologise for my behaviour last night.'

'Thank you. They're beautiful.' She tilted a quizzical look his way. 'Would you like a cup of tea? I've just boiled your country's weird excuse for a kettle.'

Cole couldn't use the excuse that he needed to rush off to work because they were closed on Sundays and Mondays – at least they were officially, but he never took the full two days off. There was always paperwork to catch up on and he often took advantage of the quiet and solitude to work on new flavour ideas or marketing strategies. Thinking about the distillery now made his head hurt worse than the excess of Cinnamon Fire he'd drunk after leaving Belle Meade, and before his ill-judged visit to Puckett's.

'Yeah, okay.' He trudged in after her. 'Neat place.'

'It reminds me of a doll's house.' Jenna's blue eyes sparkled.

'Landon House, where I live, is much larger and two-storey, but I'm guessing they were built about the same time back in the 1870s. These low-pitched roofs and wide eaves are typical of the Craftsman style we copied from your Arts and Crafts movement.' Cole caught her surprise, whether it was the perceptive comment he made or the fact he was able to string a sentence together at all, he couldn't be certain. He hung back in the doorway of the tiny kitchen out of her way.

'This thing takes ages to boil compared to our electric ones.' She pointed to the red enamelled whistling kettle.

'I suppose for the short while you're here it won't matter too much.'

'Keen to get rid of me? You didn't give that impression last night.'

'Oh God, do you have to remind me?' Cole groaned.

'You're the one who came to apologise. I didn't drag you here.' Hands on hips, she stared him down. 'Do you take milk and sugar in your tea?'

Cole's dismay must have shown because she laughed again, a lovely lilting sound. 'We'll go with a no.'

While she was busy making their drinks, he studied her. Yesterday at the distillery she'd been dressed in baggy black sweats that concealed more than they revealed, and last night at Puckett's was something of a blur, so the tempting curves highlighted by today's well-fitting jeans and fluffy sapphire-blue jumper unwittingly sparked his interest.

'Let's go and sit in the other room … um, earth to Cole?'

He prayed she hadn't caught him gawking.

'After you.' Jenna carried a china cup and saucer carefully in each hand.

Cole returned to the living room and tossed a couple of useless cushions off a comfortable looking wing chair onto the sofa. He slumped down and stretched out his tired legs.

'Why do men hate cushions so much?' She looked amused.

'Why do women love them so much?'

Jenna's rich laughter filled the room. 'Drink your tea and let's try again. Being nice to each other doesn't seem to be our forte.'

Probably the first thing they agreed on.

Jenna's head swirled with all the questions she longed to ask him, but Cole looked wrung out. He made no move to pick up his cup, and next thing she heard a gentle rumbling noise and his head dropped to one side. It was a good thing she had little in the way of an ego. No man had ever fallen asleep in her company before, at least not outside of the bedroom. The room was on the chilly side because she couldn't work out the vagaries of the central heating controls and was afraid to turn on the gas fire. She tugged on a thick, cream cardigan over her jumper, and then picked up a red flannel blanket from the back of the sofa and draped it over her visitor.

She settled back on the sofa with her legs tucked under her and sipped her tea. Sleep had smoothed out Cole's perpetual frown, but she'd still describe his face as strong and interesting rather than flat-out handsome. A shadow of blond stubble ran along his jawline and he'd dragged his baseball cap off when he'd come in, giving the pale winter sun filtering in through the window the chance to pick up a few grey threads running through his ragged curls.

'Shit.' His eyes flew open. 'Tell me I didn't fall asleep.'

'You want me to lie?' It was on the tip of her tongue to say she wouldn't do that to him, but she already was lying. Not so much in what she'd said, but rather in what she was holding back.

'Sorry.' He gave a wry smile. 'Apologising is all I seem to do around you. I guess I didn't sleep much last night.'

'Was that the moonshine's fault? Cinnamon Fire if I'm not mistaken? I smelt it last night.' She'd hit the bull's eye judging by his sharp intake of breath.

'I can't blame everything on that.' Cole sounded resigned. 'I had some … disturbing news earlier in the evening and didn't handle it well.'

Jenna's conscience wrangled with her. She justified her continuing silence by telling herself he didn't need the additional stress today.

'I should be going. I need to move some barrels around in the stillhouse.' He heaved out of the chair and his mouth twitched with a hint of amusement as he carefully folded the blanket and placed it on the arm of the sofa. 'Much more useful than cushions.'

They walked across to the door together, and then Cole's steady gaze locked with hers.

'How would you like to go out for dinner with me one night this week … if you're still going to be around?'

'Dinner?' Jenna couldn't hide her shock.

'Don't panic, I've just come up with a safer idea.' Cole chuckled. 'Did your mom make y'all celebrate Thanksgiving when you were growin' up?'

'No, why?'

'It's this Thursday. My dad's side of the family always have a big get-together at Uncle Adam and Aunt Eliza's house. They're Debbie's parents … where I stayed last night. You could come as my guest.'

'Oh, I'm not sure.' Being thrust into the middle of the Landon family was a terrible idea.

'You'd be helping me out.' His cheeks turned ruddy with embarrassment. 'They think I'm a sad old devil who can't get a date.'

Jenna wasn't stupid. There was more behind the invitation than boosting his ego. 'Okay, I'll take pity on you.'

'You're a star.'

'Can I bring something?'

'You won't need to. You'll provide enough in the way of entertainment when you open your mouth.' The trace of a smile lightened his serious expression. 'Don't take it the wrong way, but you'll fascinate them.'

'What time?'

'I'll pick you up at noon. We usually eat around two, but it depends when the football games are on TV,' he explained. 'Nobody dresses up either. Something like you're wearin' today is fine.'

She didn't go back inside until Cole climbed into his old green truck and drove off. If his family discovered the truth about why she was here, they certainly wouldn't put out the welcome mat.

Chapter Five

Cole slipped off his reading glasses and rubbed his eyes. He'd spent every free hour since hearing his mother's news poring over the distillery accounts. Even when he factored in his own savings and the largest bank loan he might be able to pull off, there was still no guarantee he could buy back his mother's shares. Of all the people his stepfather could have tapped to help solve his financial problems, he'd chosen one of the worst. No wonder Cole had felt the need to get drunk on Saturday night.

The local craft distillers were a tight-knit group because their businesses were established over the last decade or so since the laws were relaxed in Tennessee. He got on well with most of them; they were competitors but it was generally good-natured, and they helped each other out when problems arose. The only exception was the self-important braggart Ralph Bennett, the very same man who now owned half of Landon Hollow.

Bennett would love nothing better than to get his hands on the recipe for Lightning Flash. A fresh surge of anger ricocheted through him. Sylvia had casually put at risk the business Cole had built from the ground up, literally on the very ground where his great grandfather conducted his illicit trade a century earlier. At first when she broke the news about selling the shares he'd been too stunned to speak, but then he'd verbally laid into her with a level of venom that appalled him to remember.

Cole had rushed from the room and spotted Martin standing in the door of his study, white-faced and silent. He wasn't a violent man but, in that moment, he could cheerfully have throttled his stepfather. Thankfully, a razor-thin sliver of common sense sneaked back in and he stormed out of the house, giving the door a hard slam on the way.

He hadn't spoken to his mother since, and it was unlikely she'd turn up at his uncle's house today. They had a standing invitation but always made their excuses. Cole could understand why Martin didn't feel comfortable around the extended Landon family, but his mother had never wanted to go there – even before his father died. Her reluctance had been an ongoing bone of contention between his parents, and he'd heard them arguing about it many times.

There was no way to hide the financial mess they were in for the long term or its effect on the distillery. Cole didn't care as far as Martin was concerned, but it pained him to picture his mother's humiliation.

If he didn't hurry up he'd be late to collect Jenna. Aunt Eliza couldn't hide her satisfaction when he asked if it was okay for him to bring her today. The lame excuse he gave about wanting to make amends for his behaviour at Puckett's made her laugh.

'Debbie says she's a pretty little thing and a lot of fun. You could do with a dose of that, honey.'

Cole logged off the computer and went to get dressed. Being on his own, he rattled around the large house but couldn't imagine living anywhere else. Papaw, his grandfather, built it for his growing family and, after his father had died and Sylvia and Martin moved out, Landon House had stood empty for years. When Cole returned from Washington he'd worked hard to bring it back to life. Thankfully, his father's will was very specific and the house belonged to Cole outright, so at least Martin couldn't sell that out from under him.

He tugged on his UT sweatshirt – the bright orange and white colours of his college could never be called subtle – and a decent pair of jeans. Cole raked a comb through his hair and reluctantly conceded his mother was right; he needed to fit in a haircut before he turned into a yeti. He cursed when the doorbell rang – he needed to leave soon and pick up Jenna.

'Mom …' His annoyance died away. Sylvia's immaculate make-up did little to conceal the exhaustion shadowing her eyes.

'Happy Thanksgiving!' She held out a foil-covered dish. 'Betty made you a chocolate pie.'

‘Awesome. Come in.’

‘Are you heading off to Adam and Eliza’s soon?’

‘Yeah, but that’s okay. You know they’re easy about when folks turn up.’ He encouraged her inside. ‘Coffee?’

‘No, I can’t stop long or Martin will worry.’ Sylvia plucked at her gold bracelet crammed with heavy charms that dwarfed her slender hand. ‘I couldn’t let things be this way between us. Not at Thanksgiving.’ Her voice cracked. ‘I hate what I’ve done to spoil everything.’

‘It wasn’t your fault, and it’ll work out okay.’

‘You’re a good boy.’ Tears shimmered in her sad eyes. ‘I know it was hard on you when I married Martin but … I’m not one of these wonderful independent women. I couldn’t cope alone after your daddy passed.’

He could have asked why it had to be Martin Buchanan, but that was water under the bridge now. ‘How are you goin’ to manage?’

‘We’ll have to cut back drastically. The country club and golf club memberships, symphony season tickets, that sort of thing.’ A tightness settled around her jaw. ‘None of those thing should matter but …’

‘They do. Especially to Martin.’

Her head drooped. ‘This is killing him.’

‘Where will you live?’

‘We still own a small rental property on the outskirts of Franklin and the lease is up at the end of the year. We’ll move in there.’

‘There’s plenty of room here.’ When he blurted out the offer his mother’s jaw dropped. ‘The guest suite extension I built out behind the dining room is yours if you want it. It’s pretty much self-contained, except we’d have to share a kitchen.’

‘Oh, Cole, honey, it wouldn’t work.’ She patted his arm. ‘It’s sweet of you to offer and if we ...’

'Are desperate you'll take me up on it?' He finished the sentence for her. 'I understand it's not what any of us wants, but it is an option.' The grandfather clock by the fireplace chimed twelve and he inadvertently let out a groan. 'Sorry, I was supposed to pick a friend up at noon.'

'A young lady?'

'Well, yeah.' He didn't volunteer any more information.

'I look forward to meeting her.'

Cole didn't react. 'Why don't you come over one day next week and we'll hash out the distillery problem in more detail?' He struggled to sound amenable. 'Bring Martin too.'

'We will. I'd better be going.'

'Thank Miss Betty for the pie.' He was afraid to ask what would happen to the woman who was more of a friend than an employee. Once his mother left he got himself together and headed off to Jenna's, ready to grovel. Again.

Another day. Another bunch of flowers. A red-faced Cole on her doorstep. This was becoming a habit.

'Sorry I'm late. My mom turned up unexpectedly as I was ready to leave.'

'There's honestly no need to keep the florists in business this way.'

His colour deepened. 'They're from my garden this time. That explains the shagginess of the arrangement and lack of a fancy bow. These are usually done flowerin' for the year by now, but I found these clingin' on in one of the shadier spots.'

Cole followed her inside while she found a vase and arranged the cheery purple asters.

'You don't need to apologise for spending time with your mum.'

'We had a bit of an argument the other day.' He shrugged. 'It's complicated.'

'There's no need to explain.' Jenna sensed his relief. 'Why don't we get going? You can give me the condensed version of who I'm likely to meet on the way.' She grabbed her red leather handbag and the hostess gift she had ready. 'I couldn't come empty-handed. It's only a box of Cornish fudge I brought with me.'

'They'll love that. The Landons all have a sweet tooth.'

It was on the tip of her tongue to tease Cole and ask how sweet he was but his dark eyes swept over her, taking her breath away.

'I like the boots.'

She'd paired her new purchase with slim-fitting, black jeans and a soft, pearl-grey shirt. 'Debbie talked me into buying them. I was afraid they might be too much with my hair.'

'Not at all.' His voice turned to gravel. 'It's a good thing you won't be walkin' far today or you'd likely suffer. They usually rub rookie cowboy boot wearers 'til they're broken in because people aren't used to the shape compared to regular shoes.'

'You're not a fan?'

'I wore them some as a kid but grew out of the habit when I moved away for a few years and haven't picked it back up. You ready? My car's outside.'

'Come on.' Jenna locked the door behind them. 'Wow, aren't we being fancy today?' Instead of his old truck, a gleaming black Porsche was parked by the front gate. 'Very pretty. Have you had it long?'

He gave her a sheepish grin and opened the passenger door for her. 'I bought it a couple of years ago when it was my thirty-fifth birthday and the distillery hit a quarter-million in sales for the first time. I'm probably gonna sell it soon.' Cole's expression turned dark, and she knew not to ask any further questions.

'Let's enjoy it while we can.' She climbed in and ran her hand over the smooth leather. 'Beautiful.'

'Yeah.' He struggled to smile. 'It's only a five-minute drive so I'll run through as much as I can about the Landon mob so you won't be too much at a loss.' Cole revved the engine and shot off down the road. 'Growin' up I spent almost as much time over there playin' with my cousins as I did at my own home.'

A pang of guilt shot through her. Jenna could probably recite the Landon family tree off by heart, but she settled her face in an interested expression and let him talk. Adam was his late father's younger brother and he and his wife Eliza had five children. Debbie was the youngest and the only one still living at home. Her four brothers were all married with families of their own and the eight grandchildren ranged from a brand new baby girl up to a couple of teenage boys.

'My grandmother, Barbara, lives with my aunt and uncle too, and she's a real special lady. We all call her Mimi.' His face softened. 'She and my Papaw lived in Landon House until my folks married when they insisted they didn't need all that space and passed it on. They built a smaller house on a plot of land they bought closer to town, then a few years ago her arthritis got worse and she couldn't manage on her own, so she moved in with Adam and Eliza.' Cole glanced over at Jenna. 'I'd love to hear about your family sometime.'

'Of course, when we've more time.' *Not something she planned to rush into.* 'It's beautiful here.' She admired the lush, green sprawling countryside.

'Yeah, it's hard to believe we're only about forty minutes from Nashville. It's changed a bunch since I grew up here, although there're still a lot of horse farms as there always have been. A lot of big name country music folk make their homes here now, so many of what you assume are regular barns are actually music studios.' He nodded to a red wood structure on their right with a huge American flag painted on one side. 'Uncle Adam's construction business specialises in barns and that's one of his. He does other work too – we built the distillery together.'

Jenna's anxiety bubbled back up when he put his turn signal on by a wide set of gateposts, with a pink metal mailbox shaped like a pig outside, and turned into a wide gravel drive. Although he didn't know it, their tentative relationship was on borrowed time, and if things went wrong today that could be the end. Maybe that was better than getting any deeper, personally speaking, with Cole Landon.

Chapter Six

If he pushed his worries about the distillery aside, this was a damn near perfect day. Tennessee's unpredictable weather meant that they could celebrate Thanksgiving with snow on the ground or mild and sunny like today. The kids were all playing outside and the basketball hoop in the driveway was earning its keep. Cole plucked another soda out of the cooler and tilted his cap to keep the afternoon sun out of his eyes.

'I'm surprised you aren't watching the football today, but I guess you've got prettier things to rest your eyes on.' Mimi settled down next to him and nodded toward Jenna. She'd been corralled by his aunt and several of his female relatives and whisked out of his reach. 'Everyone likes her.'

'And you don't?'

'I wouldn't say that.' His grandmother rocked back and forth.

'So what would you say?'

'She doesn't talk much about where she's from and who her people are. You aren't curious?' Mimi gave him a questioning look.

'I met her on Saturday and it's only Thursday today. Give her a break … and me.'

'Sorry.'

'No you're not.' Cole grinned. 'You're forgiven. I know you can't help it.'

'Help me on inside. Eliza will start rounding up everyone for the meal soon, and I don't want to get trampled by those ruffians.' An indulgent smile lit up her face. Family was everything to her.

He offered her his arm and they strolled in together. 'Will you be okay now? I should rescue Jenna.'

'I'm fine. Be careful, Cole. That's all I'm sayin'.'

'Thanks for caring.' He kissed her soft, wrinkled cheek and the familiar scent of lavender enveloped him. She dried bunches every year from the patch of garden she still worked and sewed cotton pouches filled with the fragrant herb to layer between her clothes.

For a few seconds he watched Jenna as she tilted back her head to catch something Debbie was saying and the sunlight set fire to her hair. It brought back the crass remark he'd made at Puckett's and stirred him again now. Cole glanced away and spotted his uncle outside the back door. Uncle Adam grasped the thick rope hanging down from an old brass bell and rang it several times. That was the signal to come and eat.

'Right, y'all, I'm sure you've talked Jenna's ears off by now.' Cole swooped in and the brilliant smile she threw his way pushed Mimi's warnings to the curb.

Jenna couldn't help thinking how much younger and more relaxed Cole seemed today around his large, noisy family. The trouble was that she felt the exact opposite. His family couldn't have been friendlier towards her, but that's where the trouble lay. She'd been relentlessly questioned, all in a subtle, laidback manner that lowered her guard until she revealed more than she had intended. When she foolishly mentioned her plan to research her family connections to the area, Eliza homed in like a dart hitting the bull's eye.

'I'll hook you up with my mom after we eat. Mimi's our genealogy nut. You should see the scrapbooks she's made goin' all the way back to good old "Lightning". She'll get a kick out of helping you.'

Cole's grandmother hadn't spoken to her yet, but the older woman's sharp eyes made her uneasy.

In an effort to distract them she expressed an interest in American history, so now she was all set to trail around after

Debbie's youngest brother, Danny, tomorrow on a tour of the local Civil War sites.

'You ready to eat?' Cole rested his warm hand in the small of her back and she felt the imprint of his fingers all the way through to her skin. 'I starved myself yesterday in preparation.'

'Of course.'

They strolled along together and allowed the younger brigade to race around them.

'Are you sure they won't eat it all before we get there?'

'Don't fret.' Cole chuckled, 'Aunt Eliza and the rest of them always make enough to feed an army.'

It was becoming harder by the minute to justify abusing the hospitality of these kind people who were making her welcome on a day that was almost considered more special to Americans than Christmas. A day to celebrate family and friends.

'What's wrong?' Cole eased her around to face him. 'You look upset.' His teasing smile returned. 'I don't do well with cryin' ladies. Just to warn you.'

'It's nothing.'

'I guess being here makes you miss your own family?'

'Something like that,' she mumbled. 'This is a lovely house. It's a real home. I prefer it to the bigger, fancier places we passed on the way here.' That distracted him enough to explain how his uncle designed the ranch-style house back in the 1970s and added extra rooms as their children arrived and money was more plentiful. 'I assume your house must be very different from this?'

'Come and see it after we're done here,' he offered.

'Oh, please don't think I was angling for an invitation.' Jenna's cheeks burned.

'I sure hope you were because I wanted to ask but hadn't plucked up the courage yet.'

'Are you two comin'?' Adam shooed them inside.

A folding door between the living and dining rooms had been pushed back to allow three long tables to be lined up down through the middle. In a good-humoured way, Cole kicked out a couple of the kids so they could sit together.

'It's essential to stake your spot. The buffet is set up in the kitchen but if you go there first someone will steal your chair by the time you get back. As soon as my uncle says the blessing you go on up and I'll keep our seats.'

Her appetite was almost non-existent, but if she didn't do an adequate job of sampling everything that would draw even more attention to herself. She waited while Adam said a quick prayer and dutifully jumped up when Cole prodded her.

'Come in with me, hon. You can carry my plate back.' Cole's grandmother was leaning against an old upright piano and nabbed Jenna as she drew level with her. The woman kept up a non-stop conversation about everything on offer as they shuffled around the massive array of food. 'I used to cook the lion's share of the food for all the family get-togethers but the darned arthritis in my hands stops me these days. Do you enjoy cooking?'

Jenna stifled a giggle. 'Far from it. Dad doesn't allow me anywhere near the pub kitchen.'

'Is that your family business?'

'Yes, my Pendean grandparents owned The Green Parrot and then my parents took over. Dad managed on his own for a while after my mum left, but as soon as I'd finished my business degree I returned to Cornwall and ran it with him.'

'How on earth is he managing without you?'

'He remarried a few months ago and his new wife, Wendy, is working with him now.' She struggled to hold onto a smile. 'I'll be looking for a fresh challenge when I go back to Cornwall.'

'Three's a crowd I guess?'

'Something like that.'

‘You can dish me up a dab of Debbie’s sweet potato casserole.’ Barbara pointed to a dish of something bright orange covered in cremated marshmallows – at least that’s the description that popped into Jenna’s head. ‘I’ll have a small slice of the baked country ham, a bread roll and some fruit salad and that’s me done. I can’t eat like I used to.’ Her eyes twinkled. ‘I’ll catch up with what I’m missing out on when we have the leftovers.’ She tapped the side of her nose. ‘I’m not dumb.’

No, you certainly aren’t, Jenna thought.

‘Eliza told me about your family connection with these parts. I’d be happy to help you do a bit of searchin’ on them. What are you doin’ tomorrow?’

She seized on the planned trip with Danny to get a reprieve.

‘Oh Lordy. Danny’s a dear boy but if you get him started on all that Civil War business he don’t know when to shut up. Come back here to see me next Tuesday when all this hullabaloo is behind us and we’ll have a go at your family tree.’

She hoped she’d get a breathing space but there was no way out. ‘That’s very kind. Thank you.’

As they made their way back to the other room, Eliza rushed over and told her mother off for bothering Jenna. ‘I would’ve brought your food over, Mama.’

Yes, but then she couldn’t have nailed me. She assured Eliza it wasn’t a problem then hurried away.

‘You sure don’t eat much.’ Cole pointed to her half-empty plate. ‘Don’t worry you can have some off mine when I get back.’ He stood up. ‘My eyes are always bigger than my stomach.’

‘Off you go.’ She cut a bite of golden-brown roast turkey and popped it in her mouth. By the time she sampled something his grandmother had called dressing – in her mind it was stuffing cooked in a baking tin – and a fluffy homemade roll, Cole returned. ‘Good grief, what are you going to do with that lot?’

By some miracle he set down the toppling plate of food without incident.

'Dig in.' He stuck his fork in a pile of the same gooey stuff that Mimi had chosen. 'God, that's good. Try some.' Cole pushed the plate her way.

'Uh, I believe I'll give it a miss but thanks anyway.'

'Unadventurous woman.' He demolished the sweet potato casserole with a broad smile. 'Do you cook?'

'What is it with your family? Your grandmother asked me the same thing.' A rash of colour zoomed up his neck. Single people of a certain age knew exactly what those sort of questions were about. Jenna rattled off the same response she'd given Barbara.

'So what will you do now?'

'I'm not sure.' She shrugged. 'Cornwall is a real tourist mecca and I've a lot of experience in the hospitality business, so I'll find something easily enough if I decide to stay in that part of the country.'

'Uncle Cole, are you done eating?' A lanky teenage boy with the same shaggy blond hair and grey eyes grabbed his shoulder. 'We're gettin' a football game goin' outside. You don't wanna be stuck in the front of the TV with the oldies, do you?'

He tossed her an apologetic look.

'Go on.'

Cole leaned over and whispered in her ear. 'Later. We're not done.'

They really should be, but her common sense flew out of the window when he was around.

Chapter Seven

A sense of pride engulfed Cole as Jenna stood next to him and smiled wistfully at the outside of his house. This summer he'd repainted the wood siding in a sympathetic shade of soft moss-green after studying up on the classic Craftsman style colours.

'It's beautiful. I see what you mean now when you described it as a larger version of my rental cottage.'

'Apparently my grandmother saw the design in a ladies' magazine and pestered her husband to build one here. They're more typically found in New York and Southern California. The Landons already owned the land, but there was only a log cabin on it that "Lightning" built for his family. A lot of the locals still call this area Moonshine Hollow; my great grandfather's business wasn't exactly a secret around these parts. They'd be sure to pronounce it the southern way though and say "Holler".' He pointed to a narrow gravel road off to the right. 'That leads to the distillery. I salvaged wood from the derelict cabin to incorporate into the distilling room.' Jenna looked pensive now. 'Am I boring you?'

'Far from it.' A tinge of heat coloured her cheeks. 'Your pride in your family shines through. I wish … oh, forget it. Show me inside.'

He didn't push her. Without consciously thinking, he reached for her hand to walk up the steps and her shy smile as their warm fingers linked entranced him. The covered porch with its typical tapered columns and exposed rafters was his favourite spot in good weather.

'Did you whip that up in your spare time?' She pointed to the wreath fashioned out of artificial miniature pumpkins and colourful fall leaves hanging on his front door.

'That's down to my mom. No doubt she'll be over with a Christmas one at the weekend. I don't let her loose indoors or I'd be tripping over baubles from now until New Year.'

‘Will you bother to decorate just for you?’

‘Nah, probably not.’ Cole shrugged. ‘After my dad died, the holidays were never the same. These days I get enough Christmas by visiting my family to do me. How about you?’ He noticed her thoughtful expression and wondered if he’d hit a nerve.

‘It was a busy time of year for my parents in the pub so decorating our home sort of went by the wayside. We sometimes had a small tree, but that was about it. I suppose that’s why I’m not fussed now one way or the other.’

A flutter of disquiet ran through him. ‘I suppose I shouldn’t be assuming you live alone but …’ Cole stumbled over his words. ‘None of my business, I guess ... but I kind of want it to be.’ His cheeks heated until he was pretty sure you could roast marshmallows on them. ‘Sorry, I don’t do smooth.’

‘That’s a good thing as far as I’m concerned.’ Jenna’s reassurance settled his nerves. ‘My last serious boyfriend had “smooth” down to an art form and I got sick of it.’ She hesitated. ‘By the way, your assumption was right and I’m on my own at the moment. I assume you’re in the same boat?’

‘Oh yeah. Mine sunk years ago. I suppose you’d say Danielle was my nemesis. That was years ago when I worked in Washington DC and it … ended kind of badly.’ Cole almost blurted out the full story but changed his mind at the last second. It wasn’t right to share something with her that he’d been too ashamed to tell his own family. ‘I haven’t seriously dipped back in the pond since.’ He chuckled. ‘I’m making a real pig’s ear of this. Let’s go inside and maybe my house will make amends for my lame flirting techniques.’

‘That’s what this was?’ Her sultry blue eyes swept over him and Cole’s urge to kiss her blossomed to epic proportions. ‘I thought your mother might have been at the party today?’

'No.' Cole snapped, his sharp reply clearly startling her. Where could he start or stop with the explanation? Instead, he opened the front door and let his home come to the rescue.

'Oh, wow.'

They stepped straight into the living area and Jenna let go of his hand to check out the reading nook next to the stone fireplace. 'I feel like Elizabeth Bennet when she first saw Pemberley … oh God, I really hope you have no clue what I'm talking about.'

'You don't want to hear that I'm an English literature nut?' He followed up the truth with a white lie. 'I'm teasing you.'

'Thank goodness.' She continued her explorations. 'Did you furnish it yourself?'

'I sure did. I read a lot of information on Craftsman style interiors and I soon discovered what I liked. I've picked up quite a few things at estate sales and I probably know every antique store within a thirty mile radius.'

'That's cool. You obviously have the same passion for this as the distillery.'

'I tend to be either all in about something or I don't waste my time with it.' As he stared into her eyes, the breath hitched in his throat. 'Do you want to continue with the tour?'

'Of course.' The muted earth shades all over the downstairs made for a restful environment and the house seemed to whisper a welcome to her.

'Ready to go up?' Cole gestured to the elegant U-shaped staircase. 'This mixture of the wood handrail and metal uprights is pretty typical.'

'Lead the way.' Jenna hazarded a guess that few women had been invited into what was clearly his sanctuary, and a fresh pang of guilt shot through her.

'Don't look so worried. I won't pounce on you.'

'Not even if I want you to?' She stumbled over the top stop and he caught her hand as she reached out to steady herself. Plastered against his firm chest, the awareness of his thudding heart resonated through her bones. The snatched moments when they held hands had given her a taste for his touch and the simmering attraction crackled between them.

'I don't play those sort of games these days.'

'You think I'm playing with you?'

'I don't know. You tell me.' His rumbling drawl deepened. 'I don't want to believe it but I've been wrong before.'

'Unless you've been in a monastery since you were a teenager, that sounds normal.' Jenna stepped away from him. 'Come on, you haven't finished – and we both know how much you love being a tour guide.' The twitch of a smile returned to his stern features.

'Oh yeah, it's my absolute favourite thing. You were unlucky to get landed with me on Saturday. Debbie takes most of the tours and she's more of a people person.'

'Unlucky isn't how I'd describe it.' She let the comment hang there. 'You should get someone else to help her out.'

'Are you volunteering?'

The shocking offer rendered her speechless.

'It would boost business to put on extra tours for the next few weeks leading up to Christmas, but I couldn't see a way to pull it off.'

Jenna was being handed the means to get behind the scenes at the distillery and possibly discover if Grandpa Jimmy's story had any truth to it, but the knowledge made her sick.

'Debbie said you were considering staying through the holidays.'

'Maybe. I'd have to change my return flight.' She snatched on the obvious drawback. 'I can't legally work here, and I know nothing about the distillery's history or how it runs.'

'You'd quickly pick up the information. You're smart. And we wouldn't pay you, not in money anyway. You've only got your cottage until the end of next week so I can trade you one of my guest bedrooms in return for a few hours' work.' Cole quirked an engaging grin. 'I'll even throw in a few bottles of our distinguished product to tempt you.'

As if you don't tempt me enough?

'Do we have a deal?' His gruff tones made her skin tingle.

It was reckless to even consider the proposition, but that's exactly how her new step-mother described Jenna when she told them her travel plans.

'*You're chucking in a good job and running off to America because you're not happy I married your dad? You'm a daft girl. We could rub along all right.*'

Life was too short to 'rub along'. Too short not to grab whatever Cole offered with both hands and worry about the consequences later.

'We do.' Jenna stuck out her hand, but he unexpectedly lifted it to his lips and brushed a soft, warm kiss over her trembling fingers.

'Great. We'll sort out the details later.'

He showed her the spare bedrooms that both had quaint dormer windows looking out over the front of the house then opened another door. 'This is my study. My father had his downstairs but the incredible view sold me on using this space. It's a straight shot from here to the distillery and that appealed to me.'

'I don't blame you.' She stared out of the window and over the long expanse of grass. A path disappeared through a gap in the trees and into the distance. Jenna turned back around. 'Are these all original?' The built-in bookcases lining the room lured her to check them out.

'Yeah.'

'Oh dear. You weren't teasing earlier, were you?' Jenna groaned. She swept her hand over the well-thumbed copies of all the classics from Chaucer to Dickens and Trollope.

'It's a fair cop. I'll come quietly.' His painful attempt at an English accent, more Dick Van Dyke than Prince Charles, made her laugh.

'If it makes any difference, the whole Pemberley thing always makes me uncomfortable. I don't blame dear Jane, though, because that's how things were for women back then.'

'I'll look forward to debating the ins and outs of English literature with you.' Cole gave her a tilted smile. 'If I show you my bedroom, will you get the wrong impression?'

'You've taken me everywhere else. If you don't, I might think you're hiding something.' Indecision played across his face. 'Mad wives belong in the attic *à la* Jane Eyre, remember?' Jenna gathered her courage and pressed a fleeting kiss on his mouth. 'Now that's out of the way, it should stop you wondering.'

'I get the message. Loud and clear.' He clasped her hand again and they left the study to go to the next room. 'There you go.'

'Oh.'

'Not bad, is it?'

A massive walnut, wood-framed bed dominated the room, softened by a dark paisley patterned quilt. The subtle sage-green painted walls reflected the rolling countryside visible from the wide swathe of unadorned windows.

'Have a peek at the bathroom.' He opened another door. 'I redid this last year.'

'It's gorgeous.' The earth-tone slate tiles, cream-porcelain claw-foot bathtub, rich walnut cabinets and cream and sage woodwork couldn't be any more enticing if they tried.

'Let's go back in the bedroom and take off our shoes.'

'Our shoes?'

'It's okay, I don't have a foot fetish.' Cole laughed and toed off his own trainers, then peeled off his white athletic socks. 'Feel the boards. Imagine the generations of Landons who have padded over them getting ready for bed or rising to start another day.'

She eased off her red boots and set them carefully next to his shoes. This had to be the most unusual seduction technique going, but she couldn't resist. Following his example, she wandered around the room and noticed more overflowing bookshelves fitted in under the windows. The simple wrought iron lamps with their plain cream shades cast a warm glow over the wood planks that were warm and smooth under her feet. Jenna let her mind drift for a few moments then glanced up to find him studying her. With two long, quiet strides, he closed the gap between them.

Cole's large, work-worn hands cradled her face as he tilted her mouth to his. There were kisses and there were … kisses like this. Lush. Searching. The kind a woman could drown in. The rush of heat as he ran his fingers over her curves almost embarrassed her, but that stopped when she felt the hard insistent press of him against her core.

'I don't usually dream, but I've been dreaming of this. Of you.' Jenna exhaled a quiet, satisfied sigh.

'I want you. You know that.' The rough growl emerged laced with frustration. 'But I don't—'

'Do this sort of thing?' She forced a few precious centimetres of air between them. 'Me neither, if that's any consolation.'

'We'll go on a date tomorrow. Something casual. No fuss.'

'Will that slow down the … madness?' She'd been attracted to plenty of men in her time, but nothing could have prepared her for this.

'It's worth a try.'

'And if not?'

Cole's silvery eyes bored into her. 'Maybe we give into it and see what happens.'

'Maybe.' Jenna's voice trembled.

'I'd better take you home now.'

But tomorrow? As the inimitable Scarlett O'Hara once proclaimed, that was indeed another day.

Chapter Eight

'Wow, that looks … Christmassy. Thanks, Mom.' Cole plastered on the approximation of a grateful smile. She had let herself in and waved a festive wand over his beloved distillery by the time he arrived at work.

'I know you don't appreciate it but your customers will, and they're the ones who matter.'

'I do appreciate it, honestly. But how on earth did you manage all this? You shouldn't have climbed a ladder with no one around.' There were swathes of dark greenery woven with gold ribbon – the distillery colours – around the old oak rafters, and a massive live tree stood right in front of where their visitors entered, decorated from its base to the soaring star in sparkling gold.

'She didn't. I did.' Martin edged in to join them.

Cole almost bit his stepfather's head off. He was overweight and suffered from high blood pressure – a recipe for disaster – but something about Martin's grey, strained features stopped him opening his big mouth.

'And yes, I shouldn't have done it either.' He nodded at Sylvia. 'She's already given me an earful.'

'Quite right too, you silly man.'

A tremor rippled through her voice and Cole guessed she was thinking about his father. Becoming a widow for the second time wasn't top of her to-do list.

'Come and see the tasting room and store.'

This time he was more prepared. The rafters were draped in the same way and pots of creamy white poinsettias were dotted around with gold glitter sprinkled on the flowers. A large bough of mistletoe hung over the tasting bar; an addition he wasn't sure Debbie would welcome. 'Wow that sure looks pretty. Thank you … both.' His decision to include Martin made them both smile.

‘I know this doesn’t make up for the mess I’ve dropped you in.’ His stepfather looked grim. ‘We still need to talk about that.’

‘Why don’t you go wait in my office? I need to check on production and sort out a few things. I’ll be maybe twenty minutes max.’ He struggled not to look as gloomy as he felt. ‘If you can get the coffee pot goin’ by then I’d appreciate it.’ With a sense of relief he pushed open the heavy oak door and his favourite scent in the whole world enveloped him. Some people found it overpowering but, for Cole, one sniff of the aromatic air and things were right again in his world. He refused to contemplate sharing this with Ralph Bennett. The legacy of ‘Lightning’ Landon had laid dormant for three generations until Cole revived it, and now he’d do whatever was necessary to save this precious heritage for his own children. Spending time with his extended family at Thanksgiving had given him a jolt, and he’d come to the sobering conclusion that being a lone wolf wasn’t working for him any longer.

His body briefly stirred thinking about Jenna. *Later*. Time to get to work.

Jenna discovered Barbara had been both right and wrong. Danny Landon could certainly talk the hind legs off a donkey when it came to Franklin’s role in the American Civil War, but his enthusiasm was infectious. The pale, wintery sunshine helped because the mild temperatures made it pleasant to be outside and meant she only needed a light denim jacket over her thin, long-sleeved navy shirt.

She’d had the crazy idea that going out for the day would be a distraction from her upcoming date with Cole, but when Danny arrived to pick her up he blew that out of the water. Yesterday it hadn’t registered how strong the Landon genes were in the two cousins. They were ten years apart in age, but the younger man had the same lanky build, wiry blond hair and silver-grey eyes.

'Are you ready for a bite of lunch?' Danny finished taking a close-up photo of bullet holes in the wall of the farm office building. 'I thought we'd get something before we head over to the Carnton Plantation.'

It gave her the shivers when they arrived at the Carter House and he told her about the Battle of Franklin where five thousand soldiers died in five hours. The Carter family and many of their neighbours hid in the basement while the battle raged around them. His evocative storytelling had a far more powerful effect on her than the film they watched inside the old house. Jenna found history resonated far more with her through stories about real people.

'I certainly am. I love to try local foods when I travel so you choose where we go.' Her permissive statement made his eyes shine.

'You might regret giving a Landon man that sort of freedom.' Danny's warm chuckle eased the sombreness of their surroundings.

Jenna remembered his cousin's smouldering suggestion the previous night.

'Cole's a good guy.' She must have looked startled because he suddenly looked uncomfortable. 'I don't mean to get personal, ma'am.'

'That's okay, and please don't turn polite on me.' No doubt this affable man was a scout for his curious family, and it was a wise assumption to make that everything she said would find its way back to them all. 'Let's eat.'

'Moe's Barbecue Café is a few minutes back down the road. We'll go there.' A shadow flitted over his face. 'You're not one of those … um … vegetarians? Not that there's anything wrong with that. Debbie dabbles with it off and on when she's trying to lose a few pounds, but then Mama cooks up a big ole roast and she forgets it.' Danny's voice trailed away.

She stamped down the urge to toy with him. 'No, you're good. I've heard it's quite a thing here.'

'Yeah, everyone has their favourite place and they'll argue 'bout it 'til the cows come home, or pigs in this case.'

There were no more inquisitive questions over lunch because they were too busy eating. The pulled pork sandwich with spicy barbecue sauce and crisp dill pickle slices should have been enough for two people, but Jenna polished it off with no trouble along with a scoop of vinegary coleslaw and bowl of black-eyed peas flavoured with country ham.

'Carnton next stop?'

'Yes, then I ought to get back to Leiper's Fork. I'm going out tonight.' She felt her colour rise. 'It's good of you to spend your day off showing me all this. When are you on duty again?' He was a local sheriff's deputy, which sounded like something from the Wild West to her, but Danny assured her that he was basically a regular police officer.

'Not until Wednesday night.' He grinned. 'I'll be working the Christmas tree lighting in downtown Franklin next Friday evening. You should get Cole to bring you.'

So much for keeping their relationship under the radar. 'We'll see.' She slipped her jacket back on. 'Ready?'

An hour later she clutched her purchase from the Carnton gift shop; a fictionalised account of Carrie McGavock's life. She was drawn to it after hearing Danny's poignant story about the indomitable matriarch of the Carnton Plantation who became a Civil War version of Florence Nightingale during the Battle of Franklin. She'd turned the beautiful mansion into a temporary field hospital when the fierce battle raged only a mile or so away, and the worn floorboards were still stained with blood from the bodies that had laid there.

'She was quite a lady.' Danny sounded sombre as they wandered along the faded brick walkways through the cemetery close to the house, built on land donated by the family after the war. 'I never quite get people who aren't interested in history. It's us. It's who we are. Where we come from. The good and the bad. Learn from it and make the future better.'

She almost blurted out that that was one of the reasons she was visiting this particular part of Tennessee but bottled out. 'You're absolutely right.'

'I'll take you home now.'

The Landon men were always saying that to her.

For the first time since the grim discussion with his mother and Martin that morning, Cole's spirits lifted to a notch above miserable. If he didn't kick it up higher than this Jenna would regret their date. The brief flicker of sympathy he felt for his stepfather evaporated when the full extent of Martin's financial mismanagement became clear. Over the years, he had leeched away Sylvia's money to pay for the extravagant lifestyle his stockbroker's salary couldn't stretch to.

'Ralph Bennett's not a bad guy and his Trace Distillery is doing well. He might give this place a shot in the arm.'

Martin's dismissive attitude towards Cole's achievements forced him to grit his teeth when he saw his mother's eyes swimming with tears.

'Ralph says he'll leave you to run things as they are until the New Year, then you'll have to get together and sort out where he can fit into the business.'

Cole had tried to be grateful for the reprieve. He towelled himself dry and debated what to wear. Last night he'd told her they'd do something casual so would stick to jeans and another sweatshirt. He splashed on a touch of cologne and ran a comb through his newly cropped off hair. At the barber's shop earlier he'd almost texted a picture to his mother to prove he didn't always ignore her advice.

The five-minute drive to pick up Jenna wasn't long enough to settle his nerves. They hadn't jangled this bad since he was fifteen and had finally plucked up the courage to ask out Mary Kay Williams, who naturally turned him down before the words left his mouth.

He parked outside Jenna's cottage and, before he was halfway up the short path, she flung open the front door. Cole's tongue filled his mouth like a ball of cotton wool, and instead of managing any sort of suave compliment he salivated like a dog over a juicy T-bone steak. Not a comparison he intended on repeating to Jenna. She'd shaken her hair out of yesterday's thick plait and the mass of red-gold waves tumbled around her shoulders.

'Do I have something stuck between my teeth?'

Cole shook his head.

'Uh, well okay. I'm ready to go if you are?'

'Sure. We're goin' to my favourite barbecue joint in Franklin if that's okay?'

Jenna turned pink. 'Not Moe's by any chance?'

'Yes, how did you guess?' It was impossible not to laugh when she explained. 'Great minds think alike. Landon ones at least. And I'm guessin' you're still pretty full from lunchtime?'

'I'm afraid so.'

'There are plenty of other restaurants around here with lighter menus or … I could whip us up something at my place?'

'I assume that means you can cook – you know my kitchen skills are non-existent.'

'Yeah, I'm a decent enough cook. If I wasn't, I'd have starved by now or spent all my money on restaurants and takeaways.'

'Let's go then so you can show off your … skills.' Her sparkling eyes challenged him.

'Be careful what you ask for.'

'If you don't ask, you don't get.'

'Jenna, you're killin' me.' Cole grabbed her hand.

'That's certainly not the plan.'

Asking her to spell out the plan would be disastrous, so he hurried her into his car and whisked her down the back roads to his house. The split second he got her inside, Cole toed the door closed and yanked her into his arms. He dragged his mouth over hers in a deep, teasing kiss before forcing himself to stop and remember some semblance of good manners.

'If you're hungry, I'll fix you some food.'

'Oh Cole, surely we're old enough not to have to pretend?' Her frank smile eased the nervous tangle in his stomach. 'Last night, in your *seriously* gorgeous bedroom, you floated the idea of giving into this … thing ... between us and seeing what happened.'

'Seriously gorgeous, eh?' He trailed a finger around her lush mouth. 'I'm game if you are?'

'Game, set and match. We win.' Jenna's breathy response made his body hum with anticipation. She stepped back, twined her hands with his and nodded towards the stairs.

Cole didn't need to be told twice.

Chapter Nine

Jenna stretched out in the bed, making sure not to bump Cole and wake him. At least not until she chose to. She felt the satisfying pull of muscles that hadn't been tested in a long time. Gentle and exploratory the first time they came together, Jenna experienced the full measure of Cole when he reached for her in the middle of the night. His breath set fire to the back of her neck as he begged her to love him again. Begging wasn't necessary. Normally she sought her personal space after lovemaking, but when his warm, hair-roughened body wrapped around hers, Jenna experienced no desire to push him away.

'Good morning, beautiful.' His sleep-heavy gaze rested on her. 'Come here.'

'What for?'

Cole's warm, rumbling laugh filled the air. 'Can't imagine.' He raised up on his elbows and a teasing smile creased his handsome face. 'I'll show you, if you're at all interested.'

Jenna let her eyes drop. 'Well, you're *definitely* interested.'

'It's impossible for men to hide.'

'Must be disconcerting at times.'

He chuckled. 'Disconcerting? Never heard an erection described that way before.' Cole stroked down from her throat, heating her skin on contact. 'Of course, women can't hide it either. Not if a man knows how to read the signs.'

'We both know you're a great reader and have an extensive library.'

'I'm interested in volume three of the encyclopaedia Jenna.' With a laugh, he flipped her down on the bed and eased back into her with a satisfied sigh.

Much later they woke up to the sound of both their stomachs rumbling.

'Is this the part where you finally feed me?'

‘Happy to oblige.’ He toyed with her hair. ‘I’d offer breakfast in bed, but downstairs might be wiser so we can have “The Talk”.’

‘The Talk?’

‘Yeah. From my experience, women always expect that.’ A trickle of frustration crept into his raspy voice.

‘Is that the “what did this mean to you and where are we going next” bit?’ She kept her tone neutral but resented being lumped together with the other women in his past. Of course, if he knew the truth behind her visit to Tennessee, he would realise there could never be any sort of ‘next’ for them anyway.

Cole puffed out an aggravated groan. ‘Now I’ve upset you. Why didn’t I keep my big mouth shut?’

‘And wait for me to pester you with questions you don’t want to answer? I’d rather you were honest.’

‘Really?’ The familiar frown settled back between his eyes. ‘People who say that usually mean the exact opposite.’ He reached for his abandoned sweatshirt on the floor and dragged it over his head.

Jenna almost reached over to smooth down his newly cropped off hair but kept her hands to herself.

‘Come down when you’re ready.’ He yanked on his jeans. ‘If you want a shower, there are plenty of clean towels in the bathroom.’

Under the circumstances, it was completely irrational that his words had upset her so much. She kept her eyes fixed on the bed and didn’t dare to look up again until she heard the bedroom door close behind him.

Why am I such an ass? Cole slammed around the kitchen, going through the motions of cooking food they surely wouldn’t eat. The coffee dripping into the glass carafe was as black as his altered mood. This morning when he woke up to the sight of

Jenna, gloriously naked and smiling seductively at him, Cole never intended to hold back on discussing his feelings with her until she unintentionally jabbed his button.

Jenna glided into the kitchen, bringing with her a drift of spicy bergamot and cinnamon from his shower soap. He imagined her face must hurt with her hair ruthlessly pulled back in a tight plait.

'I hope you don't mind, but I pinched a clean T-shirt from your drawer. I didn't feel like putting yesterday's clothes back on yet.' A miniscule smile twitched the corners of her mouth. 'Of course, I'll have to endure them for the walk of shame back to my cottage later. It's a good thing I don't know any of the neighbours.'

'Yeah, no problem.' *Liar*. The thin white cotton draped around her hips and barely scraped the top of her thighs; long, firm thighs he could still feel wrapped around him after last night. 'Coffee is ready, or there are a few teabags in the drawer if you prefer. Are scrambled eggs okay?' She stared as if he was speaking a foreign language. 'Breakfast.'

'I'm not hungry.'

'That's my fault. Sorry.'

'Are you? Really?'

'Yeah.' Cole dropped the spatula down on the countertop and grasped her hands. 'I sure am. I didn't mean all that crap upstairs.'

'Then why say it?'

'Because I'm scared, okay?' He caught his breath. 'I've a lot goin' on at the distillery. Stuff I can't explain right now. I'm not sure there's space in my head for—'

'A stroppy, demanding Brit?'

'Hey, you're part southern too, don't forget.' For a second she looked like she was about to speak but nothing came out, so he struggled to give some sort of explanation without mentioning his financial problems. ‘Things should let up when the holidays are over.’

‘Do you still want my help with the tours? There’s nothing stopping us being friends … with benefits.’ She gave him a small smile. ‘That way we can have “The Talk” later. Much later.’

Jenna’s generosity floored him. ‘Awesome.’

‘A man of few words.’ Her cheeks turned bright pink. ‘Except when you’re making love – then you’re extremely eloquent. That was a compliment, in case you wondered.’

‘Oh, right.’

‘It’s extremely sexy.’

Now Cole’s face lit up like a flaming beacon. ‘It’s me. That’s all.’

‘I like it.’

Most young children believed that Christmas was a magical time of year, so was it ridiculous for him to hope they might get their own festive miracle?

‘I usually get to Landon Hollow no later than eight when the production crew start work. There’s always a lot to do before we open to the public at ten o’clock. You’ll come with me?’ he asked.

‘I need to make a quick run back to my place first so I can change.’ The pink circles on her cheeks widened. ‘Debbie’s working today, right?’

‘Yeah.’

‘Well, unless you want our sex life advertised to your whole family, I need to look somewhat less … ravished.’

‘Dangerous word to use.’ Cole checked the time on his phone. ‘We have plenty of time.’

‘What for?’

He grinned and seized hold of her hand. ‘More of those benefits you talked about.’

‘But I’m starving!’

‘I’ve got a box of granola bars. That’s my go-to breakfast most mornings. You can nibble one in the car.’

‘Wow, aren’t you generous? I’ll remember to pack a picnic basket next time you ask me out for dinner.’

Cole’s heart thudded. ‘Do I get a next time?’

‘Oh yes. Yes you do.’ For a split second her smile dimmed. ‘If for no other reason than it gives me something in the bank for when it’s my turn to mess up.’

‘Insurance. Good idea.’ He could say more and press Jenna to tell him what was niggling at her, but for now he’d express himself in a far more straightforward way.

Jenna’s head spun with all the information Cole and Debbie had thrown at her.

‘So, you’re definitely staying for Christmas? That’s awesome.’ Debbie’s enthusiasm made her feel guilty.

‘Looks like it. I’ve changed my return ticket, so you’re stuck with me until after New Year now.’ She caught Cole’s satisfied smile and hated her duplicity even more. The first day they met she should have laid her cards on the table, told him exactly who she was and why she was here. She could have made it clear that, even if she was right about her great grandfather’s contribution to the success of Landon Hollow moonshine, she wasn’t after any money or a share in the business. All she wanted was recognition on behalf of ‘Tucker’ Richards. That window of opportunity had passed, but it didn’t excuse her continuing lies.

‘Don’t look so sad.’ Debbie surprised her with a hug. ‘There’s a ton of fun stuff goin’ on in the run up to the holidays and we won’t leave you to eat a solitary turkey dinner on Christmas Day, will we, Cole?’

‘We sure won’t.’

'Should we get back to you turning me into a fount of knowledge on moonshine so I don't make a fool of myself … and all of you?'

'Why don't you shadow Debbie on the eleven o'clock tour, and when there's a break before the next one *you* can take *us* around and we'll fire as many awkward questions as we can dream up?' Cole's suggestion made her heart sink. *What had she let herself in for?*

'Perfect.' Jenna hoped she sounded more confident than she felt. 'You don't think my accent will throw people?'

'They'll love it and you.' Debbie's earnest assurance made her smile. 'We do.'

The mischievous wink Cole gave behind his cousin's back made her blush, and she tried to cover it up by fanning her face and commenting how warm the weather was for late November.

'It can change on a dime here. Don't get too used to it.'

There were a lot of things she shouldn't get too used to, but they were becoming harder and harder to remember.

'We need to give Jenna a distillery shirt so she looks official,' Debbie said. 'Come in the store and we'll fit you out.' She shooed Cole away. 'Go and wave a magic wand over the accounts or something.'

Was it her imagination or did he wince? She trotted after her new co-worker and five minutes later was all fixed up.

'The dark green is awesome with your hair. Only my genius hairdresser saves me from being a typical dull Landon mousy-blonde.' Debbie sighed. 'No wonder Cole's fallen head over heels for you.'

'What on earth do you mean?' Jenna stopped in the middle of shaking out her plait, ready to weave a thin gold ribbon through it; the last part of the younger girl's instructions.

'Aw, come on, it's obvious. My stick-in-the-mud cousin hasn't looked at another woman seriously since he came back home. According to family gossip, he was dating someone when he worked in DC, but Cole never brought her home here. Something must've gone wrong because he clams up now if anyone mentions it. I thought he was goin' to end up a crusty old bachelor, but I reckon you might save him from that fate.'

She took a guess that Debbie was talking about Danielle, the girlfriend that Cole had mentioned, but Jenna kept her mouth shut. She suspected he wouldn't appreciate her sharing even that small piece of information with his chatty cousin.

'We're here for the tour.' A rugged middle-aged man swaggered in and grinned around at the shelves loaded with the various types of moonshine on sale. 'This is my reward for draggin' around after Martha Lou. We've checked out every store in Franklin, I reckon.' The dark-haired woman with him rolled her eyes.

Jenna's work ethic kicked in. The fact she wasn't strictly being paid was irrelevant. She'd promised to help Cole out, and that's what she would do to the best of her ability.

'Welcome to Landon Hollow. Why don't you tell me where you're from while we wait for the rest of the group to arrive?'

The woman let out a shriek. 'Oh my God, you're English! How awesome is that?'

Maybe Debbie was right and what she saw as a disadvantage would prove to be the complete opposite. If only other things worked that way.

Chapter Ten

Cole gloomily turned the calendar page over to December. The distillery tours were fully booked for the weeks leading up to Christmas and sales were at a record high, but once the holidays were over, reality would hit. It would be a lean three or four months until spring arrived and the tourists returned in force. For the last few days, he'd thrown himself into enjoying Jenna's company and pushed everything else aside, but now his worries were back with a vengeance.

He stared at the picture of 'Lightning' Landon on the wall opposite his desk; the dark wood frame made with scraps taken from his ancestor's old cabin. If he ignored the straggly, grey beard, slouch hat and clay pipe clutched in his hand, the lean, bony face could be his. Cole clearly remembered sitting on Papaw Cole's knee on the front porch and the old man's stories were the root of his obsession with reviving the fame and fortune of Lightning Flash.

'Yeah, it was illegal back in the day, but the way I look at it is that my daddy did what he had to do. There were nine of us kids that needed feedin' and clothin'. Damn fine stuff he made, too.'

His grandfather chuckled when Cole asked how old he'd been when he tried his first moonshine.

'No idea, but probably around six months old. They used to rub it on fretful babies' gums when they was teething. But I do recall clear as day him giving me a glass on my twelfth birthday. Daddy said a man needed to learn to hold his liquor.'

Cole's father, Trey, wasn't as voluble about the moonshine business, mainly because his wife insisted that it wasn't proper for a prominent Nashville attorney to boast about having a grandfather who was notorious moonshiner. As a boy, he couldn't have put it into words but looking back now it was clear that, although his parents loved him, they rarely showed any real warmth towards each other. Their brittle politeness was a complete contrast to his aunt and uncle's openly loving marriage. Shortly before his tragic death, his dad changed the course of Cole's life, although neither of them realised it at the time. They were in his study one rainy Sunday afternoon, and Trey had unlocked his bottom desk drawer before plucking out a thin, black leather notebook and a computer disc.

'I want you to have this.' He smoothed his fingers over the fragile cover and reverently pried the book open. 'It's "Lightning" Landon's recipe book and all his notes. They're hard to read because he wasn't the most educated man, but I've translated them as best I can and put all that on the floppy disc. I reckon they'll legalise whisky distilling soon and, when they do, this is your legacy. Make the family proud, son.'

Without being told, he'd known not to mention the conversation to his mother. Cole dutifully went off to college and then on to law school as expected. In private he studied up on the art of moonshine distillation, reading everything he could lay his hands on from the chemistry involved to the musings of 'Popcorn' Sutton; the most famous bootleg moonshiner out of Appalachia. While practising dreary corporate law in Washington DC, he even fiddled around with making moonshine in the basement of the house he rented. Cole bided his time and watched as new small distilleries opened around Tennessee and moonshine emerged from the shadows.

The day he proudly hung up the new sign for Landon Hollow Distillery, he swore to make his great grandfather proud. A flicker of that old fighting spirit returned now. There had to be a way around this problem. 'Lightning' Landon didn't acquire a reputation for the best moonshine in a dozen counties by following the rules, so Cole needed to think outside the box.

Maybe he and Jenna could talk through it tonight? Was it wrong to dump his money worries on her, or would it bring them closer? Perhaps it shouldn't have surprised him, but when he hung back out of sight as she led the first of two tours this morning the breadth of her knowledge astounded him. She was a natural with people and they lapped up her wry British humour. After sharing a quick sandwich lunch at his desk, he wished her good luck before she ran off to see his grandmother. Jenna would be ready for some of Cole's special brand of loving by the time he picked her up later.

'Won't your folks miss you at Christmas?' Mimi asked.

Jenna wouldn't have been surprised to see smoke rising from Barbara's knitting needles. She'd never seen anyone work so fast. She had been told that every year Mimi's eight great grandchildren received a handmade jumper as their Christmas present, and the adorable pink, fluffy one taking shape now was sporting a purple and silver unicorn on the front. Four-year-old Abigail, Danny's little daughter, would surely adore it.

She didn't want to be rude but got a little tired of the assumption that everyone enjoyed the same sort of holiday experience as the Landons. Jenna rattled off a brief explanation about her family circumstances, omitting the part about her parents not having a direct conversation in over twenty years and the way they always verbally tore each other apart to her.

'Might do them good to miss you.'

'You could be right.' Jenna pointed to a silver-framed photograph of a smiling young man in uniform on the small table by Mimi's elbow. 'Is that Cole's grandfather?'

'Yes, that's my sweet man. The grandkids called him Papaw and he loved them all to death.' Her face crumpled. 'He worshipped our two boys and when we lost Trey, it about broke his heart. When he died the next year the doctors said it was a massive stroke, but I knew the truth. I still miss him every day.'

'I'm sure.'

Barbara peered over the top of her glasses. 'It's somethin' special to love someone that hard.' It wasn't obvious but, to her, the implication seemed to be that Jenna's family history made her unreliable. 'I'll be finished with this sleeve in a few minutes, then we'll see what we can find on your great grandfather. Do you know his name and date and place of birth?'

Eliza breezed into the den carrying a fresh pine Christmas wreath and two rolls of ribbon. 'I can't decide on red or gold for the bow.'

In that split second, Jenna changed her mind. Her deepening relationship with Cole altered everything, not least because the more she got to know him the more she became convinced that he would never have built the distillery on the back of a lie. To stand any hope with him, she needed to let go of her great grandfather's story and accept that her mother had been right. The old letter could revert to a family relic, mused over and talked about but left as nothing more than ancient history. Maybe it was wishful thinking on her part to hope that one day she could joke about the whole thing with Cole.

'Where are you going to hang it?' Her question made both women laugh.

'On the front door, of course. Don't you do the same?'

'A lot of English people do, but I don't bother with Christmas decorations much myself.' Their mouths gaped and anyone would think she'd just admitted to eating small children. Jenna tried to mitigate their shock by explaining she didn't have a place of her own at the moment anyway. 'Your door is white, so I think I would go for—'

'Red.' Barbara interrupted in a tone that brooked no argument. 'We always have red, Eliza. Why on God's green earth would you think of changing it?'

'Sometimes a change does everyone good,' Jenna said. 'Gold would be less ordinary.'

‘Is everything all right with you two?’ A frown knotted Eliza’s brow.

‘Why wouldn’t it be? We were having a good old chat, and I’m just going to get started on this young lady’s family tree.’

‘Would you mind if we left that for another day?’ Jenna asked. ‘I’ve got a bit of a headache coming on.’

‘Really?’ Barbara peered at her.

‘Yes, really.’

‘Mama! Jenna’s our guest. What is wrong with you?’ Eliza chided her mother.

Jenna felt bad, even though her headache was genuine. The previous evening she’d purposely chosen to return to her rental cottage for a good night’s sleep, but it’d been a wasted effort. All she’d done was to keep going over all the information she needed to take her first solo groups around the distillery that morning.

‘Would you like a couple of ibuprofen, hon?’

‘No thanks. I had a bit of a restless night, so I’ll go on back to my cottage and take a nap.’

‘You do look a bit peaky.’ Barbara frowned at her. ‘Come over again any time.’

She thanked them and endured tight hugs she didn’t deserve before hurrying outside to her car. Jenna flopped behind the wheel as a text from Cole popped onto her phone.

I need to pick your brain tonight so you can help me with a problem. More important I just want to be with you again. Pick you up at six?

She traced her finger over the screen and a tiny sigh escaped her lips before she responded in the affirmative with a trail of smiley heart emojis.

Cole set the battered cardboard box down on the kitchen table and dusted it off. He felt Jenna’s sympathetic gaze resting on him as he gathered the courage to look inside. When they'd talked about whether or not they put up Christmas decorations it had set him thinking, and a quick phone call to his mom confirmed his suspicions.

'All that old stuff? I suppose it's still up in the attic. We didn't bring any of that junk along when we moved here. Most of it was your daddy's from when he was a boy. He and Uncle Adam shared things out between them.'

She didn't need to spell out that Trey's decorations wouldn't have been good enough for Martin Buchanan.

The decades-old brown, shiny tape fell off like sunburned skin as he eased back the flaps. Cole lifted out the lopsided angel laying on the top and fluffed out her squashed feathers. When he was a little boy, she'd always sat on top of the Christmas tree; a relic from his father's boyhood. Every year his mother threatened to replace her, but his dad would laugh and smother Sylvia with kisses until she gave in; that rare display of affection between them had stuck in his mind. A tsunami of emotions swept through him and he bit back tears.

'Are you okay?' Jenna asked.

'Yeah,' Cole lied.

'Really?' Her vivid blue eyes focused on him, leaving nowhere to hide from the truth.

'No.' Baring his soul didn't come naturally, but he started with the relatively easy part and explained the history behind the bedraggled angel decoration.

'Seeing her again brings your dad to the forefront of your mind.'

'He's never far from it.' Cole shrugged.

'Can you bear to tell me what happened to him?'

'No … but I can't stand not to either.' He sucked in a few steadying breaths and appreciated her tactful silence. 'I'd just turned thirteen and he went turkey hunting with Uncle Adam and a group of guys, same as they did every March. That year Dad wanted to take me along, but Mom put her foot down and made me stay home. There was an accident. He was shot and killed.'

Jenna's eyes flared wide, and he went ahead and answered the question she was no doubt afraid to ask.

'Adam.'

'Your uncle was responsible?'

'Yeah ... but not really. The police investigation cleared him. Dad forgot to put on his orange hunting vest and my uncle didn't see him through the trees.' He shuddered. 'If I'd been there perhaps he would've been more careful.'

'You can't think that way.'

'Why not?' His voice cracked. 'We'll never know.' Cole wiped desperately at his eyes and tried for a weak smile. 'I'm pretty sure friends with benefits aren't supposed to get stuck with all this angst.'

'The important word is "friends", and good ones will always be there for each other. No matter what.'

'I'll do the same for you in return. Any time.'

'Beware of promises you might not be able to keep.' A shadow crossed her face and Cole got the sense, yet again, that she carried her own burdens. 'What about this sweet angel? You need a tree to put her on.'

'I thought neither of us were much for the whole Christmas rigmarole?'

'Your beautiful house would suit it.' Jenna shrugged. 'We could keep it simple.'

'We?'

'You've got the wrong idea about me,' she insisted. 'I'm not anti-Christmas in the least.'

A bright idea struck him. 'Grab your coat. We're goin' out.'

'Dare I ask where to?'

The Boy Scout troop he was part of growing up sold Christmas trees as a fundraiser, and the boys and their parents took turns working the several different tree lots scattered around the area. Those special hours spent with his father were some of Cole's most treasured memories. His halting explanation made her smile.

'Perfect. Let's go buy a tree.'

In the car he reminisced some more, and Jenna laughed so hard she almost cried when he expanded on his mother's dislike of the whole experience. 'Quite often it was cold and rainy, so that was the first strike against it. The leaders would make a fire in an old oil barrel and we'd feed it with branches we trimmed off the trees and cook marshmallows. Mom didn't like getting her hair smoky while listening to boys telling jokes that nine times out of ten involved noisy, smelly body functions – definitely not her idea of a good time.'

She looked thoughtful. 'Will you tell me more about your dad later?'

Cole nipped his truck into an empty parking spot across the road from the tree sales lot and switched off the engine. 'Yeah. Mom gets upset if I mention him too much. From things I've picked up over the years, I've gotten the impression their marriage wasn't the best. The few times I've tried to ask her if that's true she always denied it. The rest of the family … I guess they think it upsets me to talk about Dad, plus Uncle Adam's still torn apart by what happened.' He heaved a frustrated sigh. 'Sometimes it's like he never existed.'

Jenna rested her warm fingers against his cheek. 'But he does. He's here. In you.'

'You're right.' His throat tightened. 'They'll be closed for the night if we don't hurry.' Cole nodded towards the twinkling strands of white lights strung up over the tree lot. 'Come on, we've got an important decision to make.' As they strolled across the street, he rattled off a list of the different types of trees they'd probably have on sale. 'Dad reckoned the balsam fir was the best combination of looks and scent. Any kind of fir will work though, but spruces are a no-go because they don't smell of anything.'

An eager, fresh-faced boy latched onto them and amused them with the earnest sales spiel he recited as he led them around the rows of trees arranged in metal stands.

'What are you doin' here?' Emory Landon sauntered over from where he'd been talking to a couple of the other adult leaders. Cole could kick himself for forgetting that his oldest cousin's son, Jacob, was in the troop now. The family would lap it up when it got back that he and Jenna were seen buying a tree together – one sign of a serious relationship in their books.

'I know you're not the smartest, cuz, but let's think about this.' Cole chuckled. 'You're sellin' trees and I've got a wallet full of cash. Think we can do a swap?'

'We've found the perfect one.' Jenna tugged on his arm. 'Brandon here is a great salesman.' The young boy flushed with pleasure. 'Come and see.'

'Yeah, Cole. Do what the lady says.' If Emory's grin got any wider, his round, ruddy face would split in two.

He ignored the dig and followed her to the back of the tree display. 'This one?' It had to be the biggest one on sale.

'It'll look awesome with your vaulted ceiling in the family room.'

Cole thought of their tiny box of decorations, but Jenna's face sparkled brighter than the fairy lights over their heads so he couldn't bear to dent her joy. 'Sure, we'll get this one.'

'Wow. Really, sir?' The kid gawped at him. 'We can bring it to your house on our trailer and help set it up if you like?'

'Uh, no. We'll be fine, thanks.'

Jenna frowned. 'Is your truck big enough?'

'I'll drop the tailgate so it can hang out the back. I've got ropes to tie it down and a warning flag to tie on for anyone driving behind us.'

'You came prepared.'

'It's the scout motto isn't it, Brandon?'

'Sure is, sir.'

Cole collared Emory, paid for the tree and a suitable stand and, between the two of them and several scouts, they wrangled everything into his vehicle. Before they could drive off, his cousin whisked something out from behind his back.

'Here's a little freebie for buying this big-assed tree.' Emory waved a large mistletoe bough loaded with berries in their faces. 'I reckon you'll know what to do with this.' He nudged Cole in the ribs and winked.

He almost told his cousin where to stick the mistletoe, but when Jenna could barely suppress a giggle and tried to hide her red face, he found himself smiling too. 'Cheers. Should work for me, but I'm not sure a bit of greenery will be enough to get you kissed these days, old guy.' They were only six months apart, so age was an ongoing joke between them. 'See ya.' Once he was in the truck, he handed Jenna the mistletoe to hold on the way home. 'You know what's on your agenda tomorrow morning while I'm at work? You'll have to go shopping for tree decorations. The puny few we've got aren't going to hack it.'

'Are you sure you're okay with all this?' A flicker of concern creased her brow. 'I didn't mean to bully you.'

'You didn't, and I'm more than okay with everything.' Cole stroked her thigh through her jeans. 'Feel free to bully me upstairs to the bedroom when we get to my place, though.'

'You have a one-track mind. The tree isn't going to walk into the house, wriggle into the stand and water itself, is it?'

'I might change my mind about the whole bullying thing if you keep this up.'

She walked her fingers across his leg and lingered close to his zipper. 'Two can play that game.'

Cole lifted her hand away and dropped it back in her lap. 'They can indeed.'

Chapter Eleven

'Excuse me ma'am, I've got a couple of quick questions if you have a minute?' The short, portly man with bad teeth and wispy strands of dyed black hair draped over his shiny scalp had just sidled over from the tasting table.

Jenna was flagging. Thank goodness this was her final tour of the day. It had been a long week, but they'd made it to Friday and her plan was to hurry back to Leiper's Fork and get all her packing done before Cole arrived to help her move out of the cottage.

'Of course.' She fixed on a smile. 'What would you like to know?'

'Could you run me through the sales numbers again? I was standing at the back and my hearing isn't what it was, so I couldn't quite catch it all.'

His wheedling tone made her uneasy. Cole warned her about possible spies sent by other distilleries and had given firm instructions about how much to tell their visitors. '*Stay as general as you can and simply plead ignorance if they ask for more details*,' he'd instructed.

Jenna rattled off the same information she'd shared with the group earlier.

'Not very forthcoming, are you?'

She tried to step away, but the man shot out his arm to block her.

'Everything all right, Jenna?' Cole appeared out of nowhere. Before she had the chance to reply, he glared at her interrogator. 'What're you doin' here, Bennett?'

'Taking your little tour. Free country, isn't it?' The man sneered. 'Don't worry, your little lady has your back. She didn't reveal any trade secrets.'

Other people were starting to pay attention to them now, and she decided it was time to step in. 'If you have business to discuss, Cole, why don't you take Mr Bennett to your office and I'll finish up here?'

'Thanks.'

The worried cloud he often carried around had lightened over the last few days, but now strain was etched deep in his face again. They were both keeping secrets. On Tuesday, he'd been insistent about needing her brainpower to help with something but when she pursued it after they set up the tree, he claimed it wasn't important. Something told her he hadn't wanted to spoil the magical closeness between them.

While they unloaded all of his childhood decorations, he explained the story behind each one and most of the memories were light-hearted until he lifted out a miniature orange and white football dangling on an orange ribbon. Then tears glistened on his long, dark lashes until he'd blinked them away.

'*My father gave me that the year I turned eight to remind me of our trip to Knoxville for my first UT football game ... as if I could ever forget.*'

The picture he painted brought the experience to life for her until she could hear the roar of thousands of rabid fans cheering on their favourite team and see Cole's excited face as his father lifted him on his shoulders for the long walk back to the car park after the game.

Bennett's oily gaze trickled over her, bringing Jenna back to earth with an unpleasant bump.

'I might have to take you for my personal assistant when I'm co-owner of this place in the New Year. I reckon we'd work well together.'

The only thing stopping Jenna from asking what on earth he was talking about was Cole's granite expression. *Was this what he'd wanted to discuss?* Her brain whizzed like a speeding car around a racetrack. The distillery was doing well. She'd seen the numbers. He had started the business from scratch and built it up slowly, taking care never to overreach himself. So why was he in trouble now?

'Leave her alone,' Cole growled.

'That's the way the cookie crumbles, is it?' Bennett smirked. 'Don't worry, I won't tread on your toes, pal. You've got good taste, I'll say that. She's a bit of class.'

Cole's jaw worked silently, and she sensed he was a hair's breadth away from slamming his fist into the man's smug face.

'Go,' she pleaded.

'We'll talk later.'

Jenna dredged up an encouraging smile.

Cole wished he could capture her beautiful face in his hands right now and promise her everything would be all right.

'Oi, we goin' to talk or what?'

Ralph Bennett's nasal drawl shook him back to reality. The distillery's problems could have become public knowledge if it wasn't for Jenna's quick thinking.

'This way.' Cole steered the other man into his office and shut the door.

'Any chance of a drink?'

The muscles in Cole's face protested when he forced them to move into an approximate smile. 'Sure. I reckon a shot of Cinnamon Fire will go down well about now.' The moonshine laced with red-hot cinnamon candies might smooth over a few rough edges in the conversation. He poured a couple of generous measures from the cabinet behind his desk.

'Uh, thanks.' Bennett eyed the glass warily, pursed his narrow lips and knocked it back in one swallow. His thin face turned bright red and then he was struck by a loud coughing fit. Eventually, he caught his breath, but by that time there wasn't a thread of colour left in his sallow skin.

Cole struggled not to laugh as he sipped his own drink. 'Powerful stuff, isn't it?' When he was exploring the possibility of legalising the Landon family's involvement in the distilling business, he learned about moonshine's potent effects the hard way. The unaged whisky could pack a serious punch.

'You should've warned me.' Bennett wiped the sweat off his face.

'I thought you'd be used to it.'

Not strictly true because the Trace Distillery had a reputation for making a bland product. Cole had tried their bestselling 'Natchez Nectar' moonshine once and mentally dubbed it 'Nursery Moonshine'.

'Your Ambrosia one is more to my taste.'

'We can have a shot of that if you prefer?'

'No, no, I'm good. You're generous with your tasting samples.' His face contorted in a rictus grin. 'Don't want my other half getting her panties in a twist when I get home.'

'We certainly don't.' Cole lowered himself into the old black leather swivel chair appropriated from his father's study. 'Why don't you get on with it and spit out what you came here to say? Martin promised I had until the New Year to get you off my back.' Out of sight, he laid his phone down behind a pile of papers to record the conversation. It wouldn't do any harm to stay one step ahead of Bennett.

'There's no need for that attitude. I did your stepfather a favour. Buchanan needed the money and I helped him out.'

'Yeah, buying shares in a successful business at a rock bottom price was real generous of you.' Legally they hadn't been ripped off, but it still left a sour taste in Cole's mouth. 'Let's get down to brass tacks. How much do you want for my mother's shares?'

'They're not for sale.'

'How much?' They said everyone and everything had a price. It was something he preferred not to believe, but right now he prayed it was true. A snake-like expression inched over Bennett's narrow features.

'Two million.'

'You're fuckin' kidding me.' He gripped the arms of the chair to stop him reaching across the desk and grabbing his adversary's scrawny throat.

'I don't joke about business. You want it badly enough, I guess you'll find the money.' Bennett fiddled with the diamond ring on his pinkie finger. 'If you don't, then I guess we're gonna be partners come January.'

'Clear off and don't set foot in Landon Hollow again unless you're invited.'

'You wanna play it that way, it's fine by me.' Bennett stood up, tipped one finger to his head and sauntered out.

Cole cut off the recording and sat rooted to his desk.

'I thought you might like a coffee before I dash off.' Jenna hovered in the doorway.

'That would be great. Thanks.' He took the steaming mug from her. 'I'm sorry about Ralph Bennett. He's a jerk. I promise I'll explain … but not here. It'll have to be later.'

'I'm not pushing you, am I?'

'No.'

'Good. Are our evening plans still on?' she asked.

'Why wouldn't they be?' Cole frowned. 'Unless you've changed your mind. You might not wanna move in with a guy who hasn't been completely honest.'

'Are you sleeping with another woman besides me?' A fresh tinge of colour lit up her cheeks.

'No!'

'I certainly didn't think so, but that was the worst thing I could come up with apart from you murdering someone and burying them in your back garden. There are a few more deal-breakers, but I'll take a chance on you for now. I'm off to pack and then I'll come over to your place,' she glanced at her watch, 'by about five. We'll talk while we eat dinner.'

He stumbled over his words in an effort to thank her.

'Shush or you'll make me blush.'

'I love doin' that.' Cole lowered his voice. 'Especially—'

'Behave yourself! We're at work, in case you'd forgotten.' Jenna's sparkling eyes wholly negated the reprimand.

'I'll be locking the doors in thirty minutes. All bets are off then.'

'They certainly will be.' She shimmied out of his office with her hips swaying in a tight fitting pair of black jeans.

Cole let a tiny sigh escape before he knuckled down to wrap up his paperwork for the day.

Jenna threw the last few bits of food left in her fridge in a carrier bag to take to Cole's. She made a quick sweep of the cottage to make sure she hadn't forgotten anything and loaded up her car. A frisson of uncertainty trickled through her. A fortnight. Fourteen days. Two weeks. Whichever way she phrased it, the amount of time couldn't be stretched. When she checked into Magnolia Cottage, she'd expected to spend her time in Tennessee checking out a few facts and then confronting the owners of the Landon Hollow Distillery. Instead, she was hosting tours of the very same distillery, sharing Cole Landon's bed and, in a few short minutes, would be moving into his house. It made her head spin. Whilst they were two people who were far from Christmas fanatics, they planned to drive into Franklin tonight for the city's tree lighting ceremony. The weather had turned much colder all of a sudden, so she'd picked out an emerald-green wool coat, emerald jumper, dark grey cord trousers and black boots to wear.

Jenna locked up the cottage and popped the keys back on their hook inside the garage. Along the way she checked out the

Christmas decorations popping up outside many of the houses, a new favourite hobby of hers, and ten minutes later her car wheels crunched over Cole's gravel driveway. She parked next to his massive truck, grabbed her bags and almost skipped up to the front door. Before she had a chance to ring the bell, Cole appeared and her heart did a flip before it registered that he wasn't smiling or rushing to kiss her.

'Wow, is this your little Brit?' A tall, willowy redhead leaned on his shoulder. 'Not your usual type, but she's cute.'

Jenna gritted her teeth. Cute was how people described adorable kittens in those YouTube videos always doing the rounds. It shouldn't be applied to a grown woman.

'Cole's told me all about you. I'm Danielle by the way.'

Jenna was confused. This woman was supposed to be ancient history, so why was she hanging all over Cole and making *her* feel like an interloper? She pinned him with a firm stare that told him to come up with an explanation. *Now*.

Cole turned bright red. 'Danielle is my ex … um …'

'Oh, babe, you haven't told her about us, have you?' The woman's tinkling laughter grated on Jenna's nerves. 'Silly boy.'

Us?

'I'm his ex-wife, sweetie,' Danielle trilled. 'Sort of, anyway.'

Jenna froze.

'Come inside so I can explain,' Cole begged. 'Please, Jenna.' He eased the other woman out of the way and held out his hand.

She ignored it and strode in past them both.

Chapter Twelve

Cole wished he could wipe the bitter disappointment off Jenna's face. On the way home from work, he'd picked up some fried chicken for their dinner and worked out in his mind the best way to explain the situation with Ralph Bennett. When the doorbell jangled, a rush of excitement had surged through him, sure that Jenna had come early because she couldn't wait to be with him. When he'd flung open the door he stared in horror at the one woman he'd hoped never to see again, and while he was still in a state of shock Danielle had persuaded him to let her into the house. His youthful stupidity combined with a lack of honesty had come back to haunt him in the worst way. If he lost Jenna now, he'd have no one to blame but himself.

'Would anyone like a drink?' A whole bottle of Cinnamon Fire wouldn't defrost Jenna's icy glare, whereas his ex simply looked amused. 'Let's sit down.'

'I'm happy to leave you two alone,' Danielle offered.

'Please stay.' Jenna clearly didn't trust him to be honest. A lump of misery settled in his gut.

'Fine.' Danielle shrugged and gazed around the room. 'Christmas decorations? They must be her doing because you aren't into that sort of thing.'

'We put them up together.' Cole rested his hand on Jenna's shoulder.

'Very cosy. Watch out, it's the first step. You'll be completely domesticated if you're not careful.'

Sounded pretty damn good to him.

'I'm only speaking for myself, but I'm not remotely interested in your opinion on anything concerning us.' Jenna's claws came out and a miniscule ray of hope flared in Cole. She referred to 'us' as though the two of them could still be a couple. That dream faded when she switched her attention back on him. 'I know we haven't been together long but I find it … curious, is the politest way to phrase it … that when we swapped stories about our previous relationships you never mentioned you'd been married before. Did Danielle slip your mind? I have to say that strikes me as extremely unlikely.'

'No.' He cleared his throat. 'We were married very briefly when I worked in Washington DC, and I mean briefly.' A trickle of sweat inched down his face. 'Less than three months. It was an impulsive thing, and we regretted it almost immediately. We never told anyone and sort of swept it under the carpet.'

'So why not tell me? I wouldn't have cared.'

'Because dear Cole is old school,' Danielle chimed in. 'Everyone in his family has been married forever.'

'So, why are you here now?' Jenna challenged.

'I was in Nashville working a fashion show and thought I'd look up a few old friends.'

'That's hogwash. We're not friends.' His declaration appeared to surprise both women. 'We haven't been friends for over a decade, if we ever were.' Two round pink spots coloured Danielle's hollow cheeks. 'Be honest for once in your life.'

'I need somewhere to … be ... for a while.' She fiddled with a massive diamond ring on her left hand that he hadn't noticed before. 'I won't get under your feet. It'll only be for a few days. Please.'

'You want to stay here?' Cole couldn't wrap his head around her bizarre request.

'Yes, if it's not imposing too much.'

'Uh, is that okay with you, Jenna?' He needed to put the choice firmly in her hands.

'It's your house.'

Cole clasped her shoulders so she couldn't avoid looking at him. 'Yeah, but I'm asking because your opinion matters to me. I'm more than happy to get Danielle a hotel room.'

'No, it's all right.' A spark flickered in her bright blue eyes. 'She can use either of the guest bedrooms … they'll both be free.'

'Thank you.' Later he'd make up for his lack of eloquence.

'I can stay?'

He'd only sensed Danielle's vulnerability once before. Shortly after their honeymoon she went into a blind panic when she suspected she might be pregnant. When she was proved wrong her relief was palpable. Before they married she went along with Cole's wish to have a family one day but, after the false alarm, he discovered that children were never part of her life plan.

'Yes, but we're going out straight after dinner.' He felt obliged to invite her to join them.

'A Christmas tree lighting? Now I know you've lost it completely,' Danielle scoffed. 'Even if I was interested in going, which I most definitely am not, you don't want my company – and *she* certainly doesn't.' She tossed a dismissive nod Jenna's way.

'Do you blame her? I certainly don't. I picked up a bucket of fried chicken for our supper. We're goin' to eat now and there's plenty if you care to join us?'

'Fried chicken? I don't think so.'

Anyone would think he offered her arsenic. Not the worst idea ever.

'Tell me where my room is and I'll get out of your hair.'

'Would you like me to show Danielle upstairs while you see to our food?' Jenna's offer made his heart sink. He'd prefer not to leave the two women alone, but she'd wonder what was up if he turned her down.

'Sure thing.' Cole deserved her twitch of amusement.

Jenna knew it was mean of her, but she purposely showed Danielle into the smaller of the two guest rooms. 'There's a bathroom down the hall but, don't worry, we won't be sharing. The master bedroom has its own.' She considered herself to be average looking and occasionally verging on pretty when she made an effort, but her self-confidence shrivelled beside this glamorous creature. She couldn't bear to allow the traitorous thought to sneak into her head that a measure of Cole's attraction to her might be based on a longing for a certain redhead who got away.

'In case you're worried, I'm not looking to rekindle anything with your man.' Danielle waved a massive diamond ring in Jenna's face. 'Leo's a wildly successful Italian businessman and in a completely different league to your little back woods distiller.'

She wasn't sure what annoyed her most. The other woman's assumption that Cole would still be interested if she beckoned her finger or her sneering dismissal of his business.

'When's the big day?'

'We haven't set the date yet.' A shadow flickered over Danielle's face. 'There's a lot to arrange when you're talking about a million-dollar wedding with international guests flying in from around the globe.'

Something was wrong or the woman wouldn't be here. 'I'll leave you to unpack.' She hurried back to the kitchen and Cole looked surprised to see her.

'That was quick.'

'We didn't have much to say.'

'Oh, right.' He sounded relieved. 'We'd better hurry up and eat so we can get a move on. It'll be a bit of a hike because we're already too late to park close, and the decent weather means a crowd of folk will turn up. Good thing you aren't wearin' your fancy cowboy boots.' A familiar tingle zinged through her as Cole's warm hand closed over hers. 'I've been a dumb idiot.

You must have a whole bunch of questions about Danielle, and we still haven't talked about Ralph Bennett. Is it way out of line for me to suggest we try to enjoy the evening and save the rest for later? I reckon we could both do with getting in the festive spirit.'

Jenna reached for a crispy chicken breast. 'Maybe I'm equally mad, but okay we've got a deal.' He wasn't the only deceptive one in this relationship, so maybe this soothed her conscience a little.

They ate without saying much and, for the first time, she wasn't reluctant to leave his beautiful house. The amount of traffic picked up the closer they got to Franklin; Cole had been right about the large crowds trying to make their way into the small, picturesque town. Cole tracked down a parking spot and they linked hands to walk off in the same direction as everyone else.

'I'm glad we managed to park on this side of town so you'll get the full effect of the lights stretching all the way down Main Street as we head down past the shops. The aim is to end up as close as we can to the square because that's where the tree is set up – and the entertainment stage.' Cole kept his arm around her waist as they zig-zagged their way through the crowds.

'Oh, it's beautiful.' She stopped after they'd crossed the road. 'If someone asked me to draw a picture of my vision of small-town America, this is how it would look.' The tree-lined road of classic Victorian-era buildings glowed with white fairy lights and, halfway along the right-hand side, the Franklin Cinema's neon-red frontage looked like something from an old film.

'Yeah, it's Leiper's Fork on steroids.' His eyes were almost pure silver as he drew her closer for a lingering kiss. 'All we need is a sprinkling of snow to make it perfect.'

A swoosh of emotion tightened her throat as the crisp air, the good-natured crowds around them and cheerful piped carols drifting out from the shops combined to overwhelm her senses.

'I'm an idiot. It's perfect already.' He looked wistful. 'Why can't we freeze time and hold on to this moment?'

'Because life moves on. If we're very lucky, what's still to come is even better.'

'I really want to believe that.'

The ribbon of doubt running through his voice bothered her but, out of nowhere, someone shouted his name.

'Hey, Cole. Did this lovely lady drag you here?' Danny swaggered across the street to join them. 'The blame's all mine because I told her about it.'

'There wasn't any draggin' involved. I suggested it. You're working?'

'No, I always wander around in uniform when I'm off duty.' Danny pointed to a large white tent set up at the next intersection and gave them a sly wink. 'Y'all should get your photo taken with Santa for your Christmas cards. Keep your eyes open, though, or you might bump into my better half. She's brought little Abi down and, sweet as Cassie is, my wife sure loves a bit of gossip. The band Jars of Clay are playin' soon and the tree lighting's in about a half hour. If you don't stake a spot now, you won't see a thing.' He nudged Cole. 'Don't worry, the folks won't hear from me that you've gone over to the light side and are embracing Christmas these days.' Danny grinned at Jenna. 'And a certain Brit. Gotta go.'

'I guess we'd better take the deputy's advice.' He grabbed her arm and steered them back into the crowd so they could keep walking.

'Who did he say was singing?' A modern version of 'O Come, All Ye Faithful' rang out from the stage she spotted on one side of the square. If she was nit-picking, Jenna would question calling it a square in the first place. There were only buildings on three sides because the road they were walking down, that was blocked off to traffic tonight, was its fourth side.

'They're a local Christian rock band. Quite well known.' He pointed behind the large unlit tree set in the middle of the roundabout. 'And that's Chip.'

'Chip?' Jenna peered at the stone pillar with a sculpted soldier mounted on the top.

'It's a Civil War monument honouring the Confederate soldiers. You can't see in the dark but his hat has a chip from where it got damaged once.' Cole's smile faded. 'These days it evokes a lot of controversy, and I reckon it could end up being moved soon. Over there,' he gestured to a stall advertising hot chocolate and doughnuts, 'is where slaves were sold. There were twelve thousand living in Williamson County before the war.' His expression turned grim. 'There were even public lynchings outside the courthouse.'

Any comment she made would sound trite.

'They've recently erected markers to put the African-American experience where it belongs, alongside the rest of our history.' Cole shook his head. 'Sorry, I should've saved all that for another day.'

'Don't apologise. It shows me the kind of man you are.'

A booming voice over the loudspeaker announced they were all set to begin the countdown for switching on the tree lights. Cole stood behind her, and Jenna relished the reassuring warmth of his arms wrapped around her.

'Ten, nine, eight, seven, six, five, four, three, two, one and Merry Christmas!' A gasp ricocheted around the crowd as a burst of light illuminated the soaring tree against the star-lit sky.

Another precious moment to capture in her mind. A snapshot in their lives. Jenna felt Cole's breath on the back of her neck and silently made a wish. By this time next month she'd know if it was granted.

Chapter Thirteen

Cole stroked Jenna's shoulder as she dozed in his arms, barely grazing her skin with his fingertips to avoid waking her. Danielle had tactfully stayed out of their way last night but they couldn't avoid her all day, and he couldn't take advantage of the breathing space Jenna had generously granted him for much longer either.

The doorbell jangled and he grumbled under his breath. Before he could drag on his clothes, a loud hammering echoed through the house.

'Someone's impatient.' Jenna's eyes were bleary with sleep when she stirred and smiled at him.

'Yeah, it better be important.' Cole shoved on his sheepskin slippers and padded downstairs. He opened the door and got the fleeting impression of a dark-haired man he didn't recognise before he was grabbed by the neck of his T-shirt and lifted off his feet.

'Where the hell's my Dani?'

'Hey, get off me.' He forced the stranger's hand loose and rubbed at his throat. 'Who the heck are you? You'd better have a damn good answer or I'm calling the police.'

'He's my fiancé, or rather ex-fiancé.' Danielle hesitated halfway down the stairs, the white silk pyjamas hanging off her rail-thin frame making her look like a ghost.

'Do you want me to get rid of him?' Cole asked.

'We're not going to let him hurt you.' Jenna appeared as well, still fumbling to tighten the sash of her red plaid dressing gown.

'Hurt her?' The man's voice rose. 'I've never laid a finger on her in anger and never would. I love her!'

Despite everything, Cole found himself believing the idiot.

'You might as well let him stay and we'll get it over with.' Danielle sounded exasperated. 'Is there any chance of a coffee?'

'Yeah, sure.' He nodded at Jenna. 'You want to help me?' Cole swivelled back to his ex. 'Why don't you and … whatever his name is ... go and sit down?'

'I am Leonardo di Monte from Firenze, Italy, but everyone calls me Leo.' He suddenly looked uncomfortable. 'I wish to apologise for my behaviour.'

'Forget it. We're good.'

'Have you two finished becoming best friends?' Danielle was clearly peeved. She'd never liked other people being the centre of attention instead of her. She swept past them all and Leo trotted close behind her.

By the time he wandered into the living room, Cole found the couple perched at opposite ends of the sofa exchanging wary looks. 'It's feeling a tad cold to me. I'll light the fire.'

'Yes, there's a distinct chill in the air,' Jenna quipped. 'I must say it's never dull around here.' She disappeared into the kitchen, leaving him to crouch in front of the stone fireplace and set a match to the kindling, concentrating for a few minutes on tending to the fire. By the time she returned, he was warming his hands in front of the flickering flames.

'Cole, I've got your coffee over here.' After passing two mugs over to their guests, she set the tray down on the low oak table and snagged one of the comfortable recliners angled towards the large-screen TV hung on the wall.

'Great.' He sunk down in the other chair and stretched out his legs. 'Okay, who's goin' first?'

'He had no right to follow me here,' Danielle protested. 'I told him we were through.'

'Then why make it so easy to track you down?' Leo's challenge made her visibly wince. 'You knew it would tear me apart when I found out you'd gone back to your ex-husband.'

'I only told a couple of people and trusted them not to betray my confidence.' She shrugged. 'Anyway I didn't come back to Cole in *that* sense.'

‘Why are you still wearing my ring anyway?’

‘I wasn’t ready to deal with other people’s questions. Not yet.’ Her voice faltered.

‘You mean you wanted the chance to put your own spin on why we split?’

Cole mentally applauded the Italian. ‘Why don’t Jenna and I leave you two to sort things out? You don’t need us here. We’ll be in the kitchen.’ As soon as he grabbed his coffee mug, Jenna followed suit and they made their escape.

‘Wow, she’s a piece of work.’ Jenna struggled to wrap her head around the idea of Cole and Danielle as a couple. ‘I totally get that she’s beautiful but, apart from that, what on earth did you see in her?’

Cole twitched a smile. ‘You aren’t goin’ to join Danielle’s fan club?’

‘I’m fairly sure the only member is Leo, and he’ll cancel his subscription if she’s not careful.’ She pinned him down with a hard stare. ‘You still haven’t answered my question.’

‘Sorry.’

‘I know I think you’re hot, but you don’t strike me as her type.’

‘Hot?’ The begrudging compliment amused him.

‘Yes, but you already know I think that. Don’t ask me to repeat it.’

‘Not ever?’ Cole’s smile faded. ‘Danielle heard about me through some mutual friends and they introduced us at a charity fundraiser. My law firm did a bunch of political work and I dealt with some very influential clients. I probably would’ve received several high profile job offers if I’d hung around.’ He looked embarrassed. ‘She saw me as the perfect foil for her modelling success and pictured us becoming a DC power couple.’

‘God, that sounds appalling.’

'Yeah, but I got caught up in the idea for a while. I could claim I was young and stupid but … I guess she dazzled me.' Cole's eyes darkened. 'We eloped to Las Vegas, and afterwards she found it hilarious to keep our marriage a secret.'

'You didn't.'

'No.' Shame poured off him. 'Doin' that to my family about killed me.'

'They still don't know?'

'No. It's ironic because they're always on at me to settle down, and Mimi's continually got her eyes peeled for a decent wife for me.' The expression on his face was unreadable. 'Do you think I should tell them I've already got one?'

'You mean *had* one.' He shifted awkwardly in the chair. 'Oh my God, that's why Leo broke off the engagement. You never got a divorce, did you?'

'No, we just never got around to it, so technically we're still married.'

'That's a pretty important fact you omitted when you hooked up with me.' A wave of nausea swept over her. 'I'm going to pack. I need space to think about all this.'

'Please don't leave. I know I should've said something, but I got caught up with us and then I never could find the right moment. I swear I fully intended to contact Danielle and then tell you everything the minute I had the situation sorted once and for all.' Cole stretched his hand towards her, but Jenna jerked out of his reach. 'Is there any hope of you giving me a second chance?'

'You don't get it, do you? How can I trust you about anything now?' On at least one level she was being a hypocrite, but Jenna's pride wouldn't let her back down. She rushed out of the kitchen and ran upstairs, completely ignoring Leo who yelled after her to ask if she was all right. The air in Cole's bedroom was heavy with the lingering memory of their lovemaking, and she steeled herself against breaking down. There would be no more 'together' now.

Chapter Fourteen

Cole's nerves felt scraped raw. After spending a sleepless night without Jenna, the sight of Danielle and Leo smiling and linking hands over the breakfast table almost made him scream. He maintained some semblance of manners and forced out his good wishes when Leo announced their reconciliation. The Italian had already instructed his lawyers to set a divorce in motion on Danielle's behalf, and Cole sensed a huge wave of relief under his ex's habitual brittle facade. Leo had bought airline tickets to take Danielle back to Florence with him for Christmas with his family. Their flight left Nashville later that afternoon so they'd thankfully be gone by the time he came home again.

Things worsened when he arrived at work. The Boy Scout mistletoe Jenna had hung over his desk seemed to mock him, and his employees were all in good humour and chatting about their plans for the upcoming holidays. When Tommy asked if he'd had a good weekend it briefly flitted through his mind to tell the truth and seek the older man's advice, but instead he lied through gritted teeth. Usually he loved nothing better than working alongside the men, but he stayed holed up in his office and pretended he had a ton of paperwork to deal with.

'Where's Jenna?' Debbie stuck her head in around his door. 'She's supposed to take the eleven o'clock tour, but there's no sign of her – it's quarter to already.'

Cole kept his tired, red-rimmed eyes fixed on the papers in front of him. 'She quit.'

'*Quit*?' his cousin shrieked. 'You've screwed things up with her, haven't you?'

Oh yeah, put all the blame on me when you don't know the full story. But he *was* to blame. Totally and utterly.

'I thought you loved her. You do, don't you?'

'Yeah.'

'Then go find Jenna, admit you've been an idiot and beg her to come back.'

'It's not that simple.' Cole sighed.

'What happened? Tell me.'

The familiar click of his mother's high heels stopped him answering. 'Hi, Mom.'

'I've been watering your poinsettias. Oh hello, Debbie. Sorry, am I interrupting?'

'It's fine, Aunt Sylvia. Nothing important. Don't worry. I'll take care of things, Cole.'

His cousin breezed off and he hoped his mother would leave too, but she pulled over a chair and settled down, tucking in her neat black skirt so it wouldn't crease.

'I know it's difficult, but you really need to change your attitude to Ralph Bennett for all our sakes.'

'Excuse me?' Cole's lingering frustration erupted. 'Don't expect me to make Bennett my new best friend because your precious Martin screwed up my business.' He slammed his hand on the desk and watched his favourite UT mug bounce and tumble off on the floor. Naturally, it didn't land on the dark green rug but crashed on the stone tiles and shattered into a million pieces.

'Oh, sweetheart. Let me clear that up before someone hurts themselves.'

'Leave it. I'll get it later.'

She looked apologetic. 'I'm really sorry. All I meant was that Ralph could make life very difficult for us if you keep up this vendetta.'

'Wake up and smell the roses, Mom. He's done that already.'

'Your father wouldn't care to hear you speak to me that way.'

It irked Cole that it was fine for her to bring up his father's name when it suited, but if he tried to talk about Trey Landon his mother instantly cut him off.

'You're a good boy, and he would be so proud of you.' She leaned forward. 'I know you lost your father but don't forget I lost my husband. The whole Landon family, especially your Uncle Adam, were too wrapped up in their own grief to acknowledge mine and they pretty much forgot about me.'

'You replaced Dad six months later. How did you expect them to treat you?'

Sylvia covered her face with her hands and her thin fingers shook as she pressed them into her cheeks. 'I did what I felt was necessary at the time and I … cared for Martin very much.'

'But you never loved him. How sad is that? For both of you.' He didn't expect a response because talking about her feelings wasn't his mother's way.

After a minute, she composed herself and arched her neck to meet his gaze. 'From now on, I'm going to take charge of the little that's left of my money. I need to protect myself.'

'That's a good plan. If you need any help from me just ask, and the offer still stands about moving in with me.' Cole hoped she understood that if she chose to leave Martin he would back her up.

'Thank you.' Sylvia uncrossed her legs and stood up. 'I need to put the watering can away, then I'll be off.' A tiny smile creased her face. 'Who's this pretty English girl I keep hearing about? My old friends, the Corbyns, claimed they saw the two of you at the Franklin tree lighting, and I almost told them they must be wrong because my grouchy son didn't do Christmas festivities.'

'She was no one important, and I'm pretty sure she's gone back to England now.'

'You're pretty sure? You don't actually know?' Her pencilled-on eyebrows shot up.

'Not really. As I said, it wasn't a big deal. A couple of dates, that's all.' Cole brushed off their feelings for each other, all the while swamped with guilt for stamping on Jenna's heart. 'I hate to run you off, but I've got a lot work to do.' Once she left, he flopped back in the chair and wished the world would go away and leave him alone.

She's no one important. It wasn't a big deal. A couple of dates, that's all. Jenna blinked away a rush of tears. After she'd left Cole yesterday, she'd taken refuge in a hotel in Franklin and spent the day in her claustrophobic room going over and over again in her head everything they'd talked about. By the time she tried in vain to go to sleep, Jenna had second thoughts about the way she treated him. She decided that if she turned up today as scheduled, it would give them an opportunity to talk and maybe sort things out. Now all she wanted was to make her escape before she embarrassed them both.

A smartly dressed bleached blonde in a black power suit and stilettos strode out of his office brandishing a brass watering can. 'May I help you? I'm afraid the eleven o'clock tour has started already, but there's another in an hour and there's been a cancellation so we could fit you in.' She treated Jenna to a gut-wrenchingly familiar smile. 'Ah, you're Cole's little English girl, aren't you?'

Did she have the words 'gullible Brit' stamped on her forehead?

The woman's low, elegant laughter echoed through the gift shop. 'I'm pleased to meet you. I'm Sylvia Landon Buchanan.'

Jenna briefly stared at the manicured hand before offering her own in return and introducing herself. She should have guessed his family would hear they'd been to the Franklin tree lighting together.

'You're even prettier than my friends said. I can tell you've knocked my boy for six.'

How did she work that out?

'He's not one for talking about his feelings.' Sylvia gave a rueful smile. 'It's one of the less appealing traits on my side of the family. He tried to play down your relationship, but he didn't fool me.'

Jenna wasn't sure on what planet Cole's harsh words would be labelled as playing down.

'I've finished taking care of the plants so, if you're free, why don't we pop into one of my favourite coffee shops and get to know each other?'

'Sorry. I'm afraid she's not free, Aunt Sylvia.' Debbie grabbed Jenna's arm. 'I've got a big group, and I need a hand with the tastings.'

'Oh, what a pity. Another time.'

'That would be wonderful, Mrs Buchanan.' She was on tenterhooks, unable to believe Cole hadn't heard them talking and come out to see what was going on. 'What do you want me to do, Debbie?'

'Pass the samples around for me.' The young woman dragged her away but, as soon as they were out of earshot, she jerked to a stop and lowered her voice to a whisper. 'You can thank me for rescuing you by tellin' me later what's up with you and my cousin.'

Jenna managed a tight smile but all she could think was, *out of the frying pan into the fire*. The next thirty minutes seemed endless as she answered questions from the voluble group, most of them revolving around Christmas traditions in England, while keeping one eye on Cole's closed door.

'I reckon we've got five minutes tops before he comes lookin' for you.' Debbie waved off their last customer. 'Poor guy looked like crap this morning. Of course I might have winkled something out of him if the Queen hadn't turned up.'

'The Queen?'

'Aunt Sylvia's okay, but she's a bit too far up herself. I'm too young to remember, but they say when Cole's dad was alive she avoided Landon family get-togethers whenever she could. I get the impression Trey was a regular kind of guy.' Debbie's smile faltered. 'He and my dad were only eleven months apart in age, and even now my poor daddy can't talk about losin' him.'

Despite Jenna's desire to get out of the distillery as fast as possible, she couldn't resist finding out more. 'I can't imagine how hard it must've been.'

'If you've finished spreading all the family gossip, Debbie, the shelves need restocking.'

She jerked around as Cole's deep, raspy voice came from behind her shoulder. She turned to face him and took in his hollowed-out eyes, his skin grey with exhaustion; she had the impression he might keel over at any moment. All of those thoughts and more ran through her mind.

'You're coming with me.' He grasped Jenna's arm.

For two pins, she'd kick up a fuss but that would only exacerbate the situation. As soon as they were in his office with the door closed, she attempted to apologise.

'Please don't blame Debbie. It was my fault.'

'Stop being so damn nice for once,' Cole growled at her. 'I'm the jerk who should be apologising. I shouldn't have spoken to either of you that way. For Christ's sake, at least let me own my miserable behaviour.'

'Okay.'

'Okay? That's all you've got to say.' He shoved his fingers through his hair in exasperation. 'Sit down.'

'Try adding the word please.' He raised one eyebrow but grudgingly obeyed, so she sat down and treated him to a sweet smile.

'I'll grovel to Debbie later,' Cole promised her.

'She's family so she'll forgive you, especially if you tell her the truth about why we split up.'

A deep groan escaped him. 'I'm in the shit, aren't I? You know the bible quote about the truth setting you free? You reckon that applies here?'

'It might, but I tend to agree with Gloria Steinem who said it would piss you off first.'

He threw back his head and laughed. 'You sound so damn British and proper then come out with a thing like that.'

'Surprising you is good.'

'Don't you think we've had enough surprises for a while?' Cole asked.

'You're the one whose wife appeared like a genie from a bottle.' The teasing reminder wiped away all traces of his good humour.

'Is there any chance you might be able to forgive me for not telling you right away?'

For a second, Jenna contemplated confessing that he wasn't the only one who needed forgiveness, but she was afraid to tip the scales away from her favour. She nodded, and his brilliant smile convinced her she was doing the right thing. Once they were in a better place, she'd do the evil deed.

Chapter Fifteen

Cole ambled into his study to set it straight before leaving for work. There were still several photo albums strewn over the desk from where he'd shown them to Jenna last night. Seeing his childhood through her eyes had given him a different perspective. The defining moment when he lost his father and the changes that had brought to his life remained the same, but she'd helped him to treasure thirteen years of amazing memories. Although when he asked about Jenna's family, she'd avoided a direct answer. He got the impression there wasn't much love lost between her divorced parents and that she was stuck in the middle.

As he closed the last of the heavy leather books, a yellowing piece of paper slipped out. Cole snatched it off the floor and smoothed out the wrinkles. His heart raced when he recognised 'Lightning' Landon's virtually illegible scrawl and hurried back into the bedroom for his reading glasses. After he'd taken Jenna back to her hotel last night, he'd attempted to delve back into the Jefferson biography he was enjoying but couldn't concentrate and abandoned it after a couple of pages.

He struggled to decipher the letter which appeared to be perhaps some sort of IOU about money his great grandfather owed. Cole couldn't be sure, but the person's first name might be Jimmy and, even after staring at the surname from different angles, he could only make out that it started with an R. A flicker of disquiet rippled through him as he picked out the words 'Lightning Flash' and 'Bubbling Bertha'.

Mimi was the obvious person to ask for help, because she spent endless hours poring over old documents in her quest to catalogue the Landon family tree. It was far too early to turn up on her doorstep, so he'd have to wait until after work. A smile tickled his face. Maybe he could persuade Jenna to go with him before they went out for dinner. If they happened to drive by his house on the way home, he could suggest stopping for a drink – who knew what might happen next? The possibility cheered him up no end.

Cole tucked the letter in his wallet and hurried downstairs. He'd ring Mimi later to make sure it was convenient for them to call on her because, for someone in her mid-eighties, she had an incredibly busy social life. He shrugged on his heavy red plaid jacket and reached in the pocket for the baseball cap he automatically tugged on first thing in the morning, usually not removing it until right before he got in the shower to wash off the lingering smell of the distillery after work.

'It's one habit I don't understand, but I suppose it's what you're used to doing,' Jenna had commented on the tendency of American men, and southern ones in particular, to wear them everywhere. 'You've got lovely hair. Very touchable. Seems a shame to cover it up all the time.'

The word touchable got to him; of course, she'd chosen it deliberately. He'd do anything to raise his chances with her, even if it took weaning himself off his beloved caps. Cole hung the cap back on a hook and left it behind with a wistful glance. The frost-tipped grass crunched under his feet as he strode the familiar path to the distillery. Mornings like this brought him closer to his great grandfather, and it was easy to imagine 'Lightning' sneaking into the woods to check on his illicit brew, stamping his feet and rubbing his cold hands together while he knocked back a warming slug of 'shine. Today the office paperwork could wait. He needed to remind himself why he'd put his private life on hold for a decade and was only now allowing himself to ease up. He'd work alongside Tommy and the rest of his men to make the best moonshine in Williamson County. Cole had picked up his father's habit of whistling while he walked and chuckled out loud when he realised he'd chosen 'Joy to the World'. Even the people who loved him most wouldn't call him the most openly cheerful of men, but the surge of optimism bubbling through him this morning refused to allow in any negative thoughts. Whatever it took, he'd winkle his mother's shares out of Ralph Bennett's grubby hands and woo Jenna all over again.

Jenna thought fondly of Cornwall and The Green Parrot without aching to be there; they felt a million miles away instead of only about four thousand. When she did return, the first thing she planned to do was give her new stepmother a big hug. If Wendy hadn't shaken everything up by marrying Jenna's father, she'd still be stuck in the same comfortable rut. Her main reason for coming here had ceased to be important because far more valuable things had taken their place. Being thrown in the deep end at the distillery, she'd flapped her wings hard at first and then soared, soaking up the new environment and people like a sponge. At the pub, her father shunted aside any ideas she came up with for improving business because he insisted he knew best what their customers wanted.

'*I've worked here since I were old enough to pick up glasses for my dad. It's in my blood and that beats all the fancy business degrees going.*'

The contrast between his entrenched reticence and Debbie's enthusiasm when Jenna tentatively broached one of her ideas was night and day.

'What do you think about serving a selection of locally sourced nibbles along with the moonshine samples and then selling those same foods in the gift shop? It would bring in more revenue and help other local artisan businesses at the same time.'

The enthusiastic young woman badgered Cole until he gave in and let the two women take a lead on it. After visiting and sampling various offerings, they quickly rounded up a few tasty things to make the most of the festive visitors. Now guests could try traditional southern cheese straws, baked goats' cheese with honey and black-eyed pea hummus with their drinks. All routinely sold out in the shop.

Everyone on the tours she'd taken today were good-natured, and the time flew by. She was even acquiring a taste for the new piped Christmas music they were using with its distinct country twang. Another of her ideas.

'All the shops play the same songs, so we could do something to stand out. I know it's short notice, but do you know some local musicians we could utilise?'

'Ask him.' Debbie had smirked and nodded at Cole. 'Any free time he gets, he's hunkered down at one of the many songwriters' nights around here. He knows all the local players.'

It hadn't taken long for Cole to contact some people and put together a collection of festive songs. In the shop they displayed information on all the artists and how to buy their music. Another win all around.

'I've been looking for you.'

Her heart did its usual flip when Cole strolled out from the distillery, bringing with him a faint hint of clean sweat mixed with his familiar spicy soap. She noticed his tousled hair was set free from its usual cap today, but she wasn't silly enough to comment.

'Do you mind if we stop by Mimi's on our way? There's somethin' I need to show her. She wants us there by half five.' He quirked a smile. 'It's Bunco night, apparently.'

'What's that?'

'A dice game. She gets together with a dozen of her church friends once a month to play. It's their Christmas party tonight, which I think involves even more food and wine than usual, but don't tell her I said that.'

'My lips are sealed. What do you have for her anyway?'

He reached for his wallet, then shook his head. 'Not here. You'll see later. It's family stuff. Are you good to go as soon as I get locked up?'

'Of course. I'll pop into the loo a minute and freshen up.'

'We'll have you callin' it the restroom before we pack you off back to Cornwall …' Cole turned pale. 'I didn't—'

'Don't apologise or you'll dig a deeper hole for yourself.' Normally her relationships with men were straightforward and she walked away from them with very little angst on either side. She'd watched girls she grew up with getting married and starting their families with little consternation. Jenna vehemently denied it on her thirty-fifth birthday when her mother asked if her biological clock was ticking but, strangely enough, after that it started to catch her out. Only yesterday a couple had brought an adorable toddler with them on the tour and the little dark-eyed girl reached out for Jenna at one point, happily nestling in her arms for several wonderful minutes. Hours later, she could still recreate the child's warm, soft scent in her mind. 'Give me five minutes.' Jenna fled before he could spot the tears welling up in her eyes. She was the one who'd suggested they needed to slow things down and give themselves a chance to consider what they were doing. Now she wondered if she'd been a fool.

He always seemed to wrong-foot himself around women. No wonder he was creeping up on forty with one brief disastrous marriage and nothing else to show for it. Cole strode through the distillery and gave his updated version of Bubbling Bertha a reassuring pat after he locked the back door.

'I'm ready.' Jenna materialised by his side and her teasing smile lifted his spirits. The shimmer of red lip gloss, a wisp of subtle musky perfume, her flowing hair loosened from its sensible work time plait; this was for his benefit. Last night he'd only risked a brief kiss, but now he slid his hands around her face, anchored his fingers in Jenna's silky hair and tugged her closer.

'Yeah, so am I.'

'That is absolutely not what I meant, Cole Landon.'

The playful touch of haughtiness stirred his desire and he tasted her lips, nipping at the soft skin until a low groan scraped the back of her throat. 'We could skip going to Mimi's?'

'Absolutely not. Your grandmother would never forgive you.'

'Fine, let's get cracking.' No doubt his agreement sounded grudging, but he guessed Jenna wouldn't take him too seriously. Out in the car, she pestered him again about the purpose of their visit. 'You're worse than a child at Christmas. We'll be there in a few minutes. Change of subject: do you have any plans for Saturday and Sunday?'

'Why? Do you have some for me?'

'Oh yeah, but the respectable ones include you getting dressed up in Victorian costume.' He rattled off details of the 'Dickens of a Christmas' event held every year in Franklin when the town briefly turned the clock back. 'There are craft vendors, various performers and the shops go all out with their decorations. The distillery has a booth in the refreshment area, and we'll be handing out samples, selling our products and generally drumming up business.'

'Sounds awesome. I'd love to come.'

'Really?'

'Of course.' She treated him to a knowing look. 'You hate it, don't you?'

'Generally speaking, yeah, but I might not as much with you there. We can go together on Friday to the fancy dress store. I've reserved my costume already, and we'll fix you up with somethin'. Debbie has her own dress that Mimi helped her to make last year, so she can hold the fort at the distillery along with Ashley and Tommy.' Cole pulled into his uncle's driveway. 'When we're done here, you can decide what you fancy for dinner.' He hopped out of the truck, and Jenna breezed right past him and skipped up the steps.

'You're a good influence on him, honey.' His grandmother appeared at the door and shooed them in. 'Normally this boy's late because he can't prise himself away from work,' she told Jenna. 'Is he a slave driver?'

'Not at all. Everyone works hard, but it's great and I love it.'

Cole couldn't help grinning.

'I'm goin' out at six so show me what you've got. If I can't figure it out now, I'll think on it some more later.' Mimi sat down and slipped on her reading glasses.

'Do I finally get to hear about this mystery?' Jenna begged.

'Sure.' He wriggled the letter out of his wallet. 'I found this in the back of one of those photo albums. It's from my great grandfather but he wasn't much for writing and the ink is faded, so it's hard to make out.' Cole smoothed out the yellowing paper.

'May I see it?'

'Yeah, sure.'

Jenna took it from him and skimmed over the few scrawled lines. He thought she turned pale but decided he was imagining things. 'Sorry, I can't make out any of it. Good luck.' She passed the letter over to Mimi and sprang out of the chair. 'We ought to be going, Cole. Someone is off out, remember?'

'Oh right, yeah.' It was only ten minutes to six and his grandmother looked dressed and ready to go from what he could tell.

'I'll let you know when I figure it out, but it'll be straight to bed for me tonight after the party so it won't be before tomorrow,' Mimi warned.

They said their goodbyes, but when they got in the truck Cole didn't rush to start the engine. 'Are you okay? You seemed a bit strange back there when we looked at the letter.'

'I'm fine. You're imagining things.'

When she leaned over and kissed him, it worked its usual brain-fogging magic on Cole. Later there would be time enough to wonder why a flicker of panic had lurked in her sapphire eyes.

Chapter Sixteen

Jenna slumped on the bed in her soulless hotel room and wished she wasn't such a coward. She could have told Cole word for word what his great grandfather's letter said, because hers was the exact duplicate and she'd spent hours figuring it out. She eased her copy out of the rigid envelope she'd used to pack it in her suitcase and re-read it.

What should she do now was the million-dollar question? Before this second letter emerged, she had decided to forget hers existed. The distillery and its proud history were everything to Cole. Jenna couldn't bear to wreck the happiness within their grasp on the basis of something that might simply be the drunken ramblings of a couple of old moonshiners.

For two long days she'd been on pins and needles, waiting for Cole to tell her his grandmother had called about the letter, but so far nothing had been said. Once Mimi worked it out, that would start a ball rolling; one that would end up at Jenna's feet. The only possible way to stop it was for her to be frank with Mimi. She grabbed her phone before she could lose her nerve and had a brief conversation with his grandmother. Jenna hung up with her hands shaking. *No going back now.*

'Off to work?' Peggy, one of the hotel receptionists, called over as she came through the lobby. 'When you gonna bring us some free samples?' The fake reindeer antlers on her headband bobbed around as she laughed.

'Come to the Dickens Festival on Saturday or Sunday. We've got a booth and there'll be plenty of moonshine to taste.'

'Fat chance. I'm working. You gonna be all dressed up?'

Jenna nodded and surreptitiously crossed her fingers. Maybe things wouldn't fall apart that fast.

'You'll be the only one there not faking an English accent.' The phone rang and Peggy rolled her eyes. 'No rest for the wicked. See ya later.'

Outside the hotel's front door the silver tree with its flashing red lights mocked Jenna's lack of festive spirit. She trudged along to where her rental car was parked and jumped in. Usually she enjoyed the drive out to Leiper's Fork for the chance to see what new decorations she could spy. People were adding more each day the closer they got to Christmas, and she enjoyed giving them marks out of ten in her head. The light displays amused her most, and Jenna wondered if there was healthy competition between neighbours to see who could design the most elaborate set-up. Her stomach turned to lead when she spotted the pink plastic pig on Adam Landon's gatepost, draped in white lights and sporting a red Santa hat.

She stopped the car by the front door and climbed out.

'Come in.' Eliza popped out before she could knock. 'Mama said you were stopping by. She's in the family room waiting for you. Let me fix you a cup of coffee … or tea if you prefer?'

'No thanks. I'm good.' Jenna needed to get rid of the other woman without coming across as rude. 'Don't let me hold you up, I know the way.'

Cole's aunt reluctantly scuttled off towards the kitchen and so Jenna took a moment to collect herself before walking into the room.

'There you are.' The old lady looked stern and unsmiling.

It might be a huge mistake to ask for his grandmother's help, but there was no reasonable alternative as far as she could see and even fewer unreasonable ones.

The women in Cole's life mystified him today. This morning, when he was eating breakfast, his doorbell rang and his mother stood outside with two large suitcases at her feet.

'I'm taking you up on your offer, but I'm not ready to talk about it so please don't ask.'

Very informative.

Debbie was out of sorts too and barely said a word while they were restocking the gift shop. Next thing, Jenna snapped at him when he dared to ask what was wrong as she arrived to take the eleven o'clock tour with red-rimmed eyes. To round things off, he got the distinct impression his grandmother was avoiding his phone calls.

He wandered over to the bottling section and lost himself for a while in debating numbers and batting around spring and early summer flavour ideas with Tommy. They made a plan to contact several of the local organic farmers to see what might be available in the way of edible flowers and herbs.

'Sounds like trouble in the shop, boss.'

Raised voices drifted their way. It wasn't unusual to hear the occasional noisy debate between two visitors who thought the other had sampled too much moonshine.

'I'll take care of it.' He strolled out but stopped dead when he saw his mother and stepfather facing off in the middle of the gift shop. 'Is everything all right?'

'No, it's damn well not.' Martin glared at him. 'She walked out this morning without any explanation, and it's not on.'

They were busy today and it was crossover time for the tours, meaning one group had finished and another was getting ready to begin. The added aggravation wasn't good for business.

'Why don't we take this into my office?' He steered them away and made sure to close the door so they wouldn't be overheard. 'Do either of you fancy a cup of coffee?' Cole poured himself one when he didn't get any response. 'Mom, would you prefer me to stay or leave while the two of you talk?'

'I've nothing private to say to him.' Sylvia stared at the wall.

'Doesn't matter to me.' Martin shrugged.

'Okay. Who's goin' first?' They'd be here all day if he didn't hurry things along.

'There's a For Sale sign in my front yard. I knew it was coming but not this soon, and I refuse to watch strangers poke around my house and criticise it.' She glared at her husband. 'This is all his fault.'

'I'm not denying that, but you never wanted to know about money. You think it's grubby to discuss the subject. I've been trying to tell you for years that we need to cut back, but you wouldn't listen.'

Cole felt an unexpected sliver of pity for his stepfather until he remembered the exclusive golf club membership, handmade suits and expensive whisky. Before he could stand up for his mother, she shocked him by apologising.

'I'm sorry.'

He might regret the offer he was about to make, or rather re-make, but it might help to ease things between the warring couple.

'Martin, why don't you move into my place as well while your house is being shown to potential buyers? It'll give you a breathing space to make plans.'

'That's very kind of you … Cole.'

He sensed his stepfather had almost slipped up and called him son. Cole had been a prickly thirteen-year-old and still grieving for his father when Martin appeared in their lives, and he'd refused to call him by anything other than his first name, vehemently insisting on the same in return.

'Would that be all right, Sylvia?'

'I don't see why not.' She turned to Cole. 'Won't we be cramping your style with that pretty little English girl?'

Explaining the nuances of his relationship with Jenna was too complicated, especially when he barely understood it himself. 'I'm sure we can work around it.'

'I'd like a chance to get to know her properly,' his mother ventured. 'Maybe we could all have dinner together tonight?'

'I'm not sure if Jenna's free, but I'll ask her.' Considering she'd avoided speaking directly to him so far today, he didn't hold out much hope.

'You could make good use of the mistletoe out there to win her over,' Martin joked.

'I'll sure give it a try.'

'We better pop back to our house to pick up Martin's clothes and sort out a few things.' His mother hugged him. 'You're a wonderful boy.'

'It's nothing.'

'No, it's not nothing,' she insisted. 'We'll see you later.'

Left alone, he stood there for a few moments, simply thinking about what an unusual Christmas this was turning into.

'We're a sad pair today,' Debbie complained. 'I'm guessing we could both do with a drink, but Cole will skin us alive if he catches us sampling the merchandise. You wanna go first and tell me why you look like you've lost a hundred dollar bill and found a dime?'

Not really, Jenna thought. Mimi might look like an innocuous old lady, but nothing was further from the truth. After putting together the contents of the letter, the family information she tracked down and Jenna's dragged-out confession, Mimi issued an ultimatum. If Jenna didn't tell Cole the whole truth then his grandmother would. The only concession she made was granting a reprieve until Monday morning so Jenna could help at the Dickens Festival, but that was a purely business decision.

'I've a few things on my mind about my family back home, that's all.'

'I bet they want you back for Christmas?' Debbie sighed. 'Mine are smotherin' me half to death. You wouldn't think I was twenty-two, for God's sake. I'll date who I want. They need to trust my judgment.'

'Are you seeing someone they don't approve of?'

'Yeah, his name's Chip.'

Cole appeared out of nowhere, hefting a cardboard box, which he set on the bar. 'Oh God, tell me you're not dating Chip Estes?'

'Why shouldn't she?' His disparaging tone put Jenna's back up. 'Debbie's a grown woman. You didn't ask your family's permission before asking me out.'

'The difference is Chip Estes is a prize idiot, and she knows it. Whatever trouble it's possible to get into around these parts, he's managed it.'

The younger woman coloured up and Jenna waited for her to defend herself.

'People can change.' Jenna ventured the suggestion.

'Yeah, but I'm pretty sure Chip isn't one of them.' He clasped his cousin's shoulder. 'You know better than this, kid. I know a ton of women think he's good-looking, but he's not a decent guy.'

Debbie jerked her handbag out from under the bar and glared at them both. 'Stay out of my business. Chip and I love each other, and we'll make you eat your words soon enough.' She wriggled into her tight denim jacket and wrapped a red scarf around her neck. 'Don't worry, I'll be here to open up tomorrow.' She left them staring at each other

'Is he really that awful?' Jenna asked.

'Yep, he's had a bad reputation since he was about fifteen.'

Suddenly, she was lifted off her feet and kissed. It surprised her for several reasons, not least of which was the fact there were several customers browsing around the shop and all of them were now openly staring.

'That's what the mistletoe is hanging there for, right?' His broad grin made everyone laugh and they got encouraging whoops and yells to do it again. Which he did, only setting her back down when Jenna begged him to stop.

This boyish side to him twisted another knife in her heart when she thought how she'd break his heart in a few short days.

The idea of leaving now, instead of dragging it out, flitted through her head, but the selfish side of her was determined to wring out every last minute. Monday was soon enough for regrets.

'My parents really want to meet you properly, so I thought we could have dinner tonight at my house … but there's something we need to talk about first.' Cole checked his watch. 'We've only got another hour until close. Come to my office when you've wrapped up here.' He sounded deeply weary, and she wished she could kiss him back to light-heartedness again. 'I'll go ahead and unload these.' Cole picked the box back up and wandered over to restock with more bottles of Ambrosia Angel; not her particular favourite, but the softer, slightly sweet moonshine was a definite crowd pleaser and regularly sold out.

Once the last customer left, she locked the heavy wood doors and cashed up the till, collecting all the money and receipts in a cloth bag for Cole. Jenna tapped on his office door and walked in, momentarily stunned by the granite expression on his face. There were no lights on and, in the shadowy darkness of a winter's afternoon, his eyes held no trace of colour, only dark misery.

'Is it that bad?'

'Afraid so.' He puffed out a deep sigh. 'You need to know the full story before dinner because it's all wrapped up with my mom and Martin. Unless a miracle happens, complete control of the distillery will go out of the Landon family on the first of January.'

Jenna ached to say she didn't love him because he owned this place, but would he believe her once she admitted the truth behind her visit here? Probably not. The cheerful Christmas music playing over the loudspeakers seemed to mock them. She walked around the desk, crouched down by him and wrapped her arms around his neck. For a moment the brush of his warm skin and Cole's unique scent, always part man and part distillery, was enough.

'Tell me everything.'

Chapter Seventeen

Cole stretched out in bed and listened to Jenna singing a slightly off-key version of 'O Come, All Ye Faithful' in the shower.

'We've only got half an hour before we need to leave for work, and I refuse to face your immaculate mother looking too ... ravished,' she'd said.

He considered it a miracle she was back in his bed again. Last night, after the briefest hesitance on Jenna's part, he'd persuaded her they needed to make a detour to her hotel after dinner, collect her luggage and bring her back to Landon House.

Yesterday, Jenna had listened carefully to his revelations about the distillery's finances and Ralph Bennett's looming involvement in the business, made thoughtful suggestions and generally lifted his spirits. She'd worked her magic at dinner, too. Charming Martin wasn't too much of a challenge, but his mother? That he hadn't expected, although it helped that Sylvia was a real Anglophile. Jenna passed every test his mom threw out with flying colours. He couldn't quite throw off his lingering guilt, because he still hadn't broached the subject of his brief now-you-see-it-now-you-don't marriage with his family.

'Shift, it's your turn.' Jenna yanked the sheet off of him and tickled the soles of his feet.

'Stop it, you witch.' Cole made a grab for her and decided having his arms wrapped around this particularly warm, perfumed, naked woman ranked high up on his list of favourite things. 'If you aren't nice, I'll have my wicked way with you.'

'Save that thought for tonight.' She stopped squirming and raised herself up for a kiss. The torture of her crisp, floral scent teasing his nostrils and the press of her against his skin was excruciating. Jenna slowly peeled off of him, looking extremely satisfied. 'I can't wait to see you dressed up as a Victorian gentleman.'

'I'll tell them to lace you in the tightest corset they've got.' He shouldn't have mentioned that because it threw erotic images into his head that made his body tighten and throb. Cole grimaced and made a dash for the shower, set the temperature as low as it would go and allowed the freezing water to sting his skin. By the time he towelled off and dressed, she was putting the last touches to her make-up. 'Breakfast?'

'Yes please. One of those awful stale granola bars you keep in your truck won't be sufficient to replenish my energy levels.' She grinned. 'As you're the one who depleted them, you can feed me properly for once.'

'Fair enough, but you've got to see this first.' He led her across the room, pulled up the blinds and nestled Jenna in front of him. 'Looks like a Christmas card, doesn't it?' The heavy frost crusting the grass and enveloping the trees resembled thick snow. 'Does Cornwall get real winter weather? I'm guessing not as it's by the coast.' Cole sensed her stiffen. 'Why do you never want to talk about where you come from and your family? Mom noticed it last night and I had to avoid a fair number of questions when she nailed me on my own.'

'We'll be late.' She stepped away.

'I know your parents split up and don't get on which puts you in the middle, but I get the feeling you're not being as open with me as I've tried to be with you. That bothers me.'

'I know.' Tears glistened in her eyes. 'Can I ask you a huge favour?'

'Anything.'

'Will you give me until Monday?'

The odd request puzzled him.

'Let's enjoy this weekend, and then I'll answer all the questions you have with complete honesty. I promise.'

'Okay.' Cole took her hand. 'We'll get through this.'

'Will we?' Jenna's voice broke. 'I want to believe that so badly, you can't imagine.'

'Then believe.' Nothing could stop him wanting this special woman in his life.

Jenna did a twirl and the dark gold satin bell-shaped skirt swished out around her. To her ears she thought her laughter sounded forced, but Cole's broad smile appeared genuine. He was either convinced or was going along with things to please her.

When he told her about the distillery's financial troubles she felt sick, because he'd be burdened with an added layer of worry when she revealed her own connection to the business. To face his parents straight after that conversation strained her acting abilities to the utmost. Sylvia was a protective mother tiger when it came to her only child, grown man or not, and it was a challenge to avoid her probing questions. Thankfully, Martin stayed on the side lines. His relationship with Cole clearly wasn't an easy one, and she wondered whether his guilt over the money he'd lost kept him largely silent.

'What do you think?' she asked.

'Beautiful.' Cole's husky response made her blush.

There hadn't been much choice because the Dickens Festival meant there was a run on Victorian costumes. Cole had reserved his beforehand, but Jenna had to make a selection from the few dresses left in her size. The scarlet one was too much with her hair and the black too drab but, just like Goldilocks with Baby Bear's porridge, the dark gold satin was perfect.

'Let's try this hat.' The assistant nestled a brown velvet bonnet on her head and tied the wide silk ribbons under her chin. 'Perfect.' She turned to Cole. 'Are you going to try on your outfit, sir?'

'Uh no.' A surge of what seemed to be panic wiped out his good humour. 'It'll be fine.' He glanced at his watch. 'We should be gettin' back to work.'

'I'll change and be out in a minute.' Left alone in the dressing room, she stared at herself for a moment in the ornate gilt-framed mirror. Never one for amateur dramatics or anything on those lines, this was the first costume she'd worn since being an angel in the school nativity play when she was five years old. The rich colour suited her and the low pointed waist made her look more shapely than usual. Cole's wish hadn't materialised because the shop didn't stock corsets; perhaps one day she'd surprise him with something like that. Jenna bit back a sob, hard enough to draw blood from her lip as reality intervened. She untied the bonnet and tossed it on the ground then forced her trembling fingers to unhook the dress and yank it off. By the time she slipped her regular clothes back on and hung the dress back on the hanger, she'd regained a measure of control again. Jenna glued on a smile and walked out to join Cole.

'Everything's paid for, so let's go.' Cole headed out of the shop. 'We're all set for a busy day. The tours are solidly booked and we need to get the distillery truck packed for tomorrow. The festival starts at ten in the morning, but we can start setting up as early as eight. Debbie and Tommy will be there to help.'

The plan was for Jenna and Cole to work the booth from opening time until one o'clock when Debbie and Tommy would take over. At four o'clock they'd be back on again until closing time at seven. She suspected they would drop with exhaustion at that point.

He quirked her a smile. 'Did you hear my folks offer to help?'

'No.'

'I almost turned Mom down but they were desperate to do something, so they're going to pop in for a while during each of the three shifts to give the rest of us a break. Mom's even coming up with some sort of costumes for them.' He unlocked the truck for them to jump in.

'They're trying hard.'

Cole grimaced. 'Yeah, I know. We're all being so damn polite, it's strangling us.'

'Better than yelling and arguing about something that can't be changed.' He didn't look convinced, but she brushed a kiss on his cheek and encouraged him to cheer up. 'What's the weather forecast for the festival?'

'It's still going to be freezing. It's always unpredictable. Over the years I've worked it in everything from pouring rain to sunny and seventy degrees. I hope you've got some thermal underwear for under that dress? If not, I'm sure Debbie or someone else in the family could lend you some.'

'I don't, but I'll ask.' Now they were out of the city traffic she sensed Cole relax, his hands loosening on the steering wheel. Imagining him as a sharp-suited lawyer in Washington felt all wrong. The distillery was where he belonged. If she loved him, which she absolutely did, she must find a way to keep his business afloat – even if it meant they didn't make it as a couple.

'What's wrong?' he asked.

'Nothing, why?'

'You looked like the world was about to end.' His silvery eyes gleamed. 'Of course we know I'm no expert on women, so take my observation with a pinch of salt.'

Jenna brushed it off and steered him away from dangerous ground by pointing to a colourful collection of inflatable Christmas decorations arranged on someone's front lawn. 'I'm not sure I've ever seen Elvis in a nativity scene before, or penguins come to that, but everyone's taste is different.'

'Mine is for you.' The quiet remark stunned her into silence. Cole reached for her hand and kept it cradled in his until they arrived at the distillery.

He drove in around the back of the building and parked, but neither of them rushed to get out.

'I meant what I said. My taste is very definitely for you.'

'Good.' Jenna croaked. She couldn't resist saying the same back to him in return. *Three more days of being loved.* It wasn't anywhere near long enough but was still far more than she probably deserved.

Chapter Eighteen

Cole fiddled with his black silk cravat and cursed roundly.

'Let me do that,' Jenna said, giving him an entrancing smile. 'If it's any consolation, you look extremely handsome.'

He envied Tommy who always played the working man card to the hilt for the Dickens Festival with his rough serge trousers, a dark shirt with a colourful bandana tied around the neck, loose wool jacket and a flat cap. By the time Cole layered on the white shirt with its stiff collar, pinstripe trousers, patterned silk waistcoat and charcoal-grey cutaway morning coat, he could barely breathe.

'Seriously?'

She finished adjusting the suitably puffed out cravat and stood back to admire her handiwork. 'Oh yes, and when we're through with the festival tomorrow afternoon I'll prove it to you before we return our costumes.'

Cole spotted a flicker of sadness running across her face. She might be thinking along the same lines as him and wondering how long they had together before real life intervened and decisions needed to be made. Remembering her plea for them to enjoy the weekend, he drew her closer. 'You don't look so bad yourself. That bustle is surprisingly sexy. Stirs a man's imagination about what exactly is under there.' He caressed her through the thick layers of material. 'You have your thermals on?' Jenna's warm laughter rumbled through him.

'For killing a sexy moment, that takes the cake. Yes I do. Your Aunt Eliza took pity on me.'

Cole pretended to check his pocket watch, a fake prop that came with the costume. 'Mom wanted to see us before we left, so we'd better be going.' He held out his arm. 'Would you do me the honour, my lady?'

'Certainly, sir.' She giggled again. 'Please don't put on that awful English accent when we're serving people today or I won't be able to keep a straight face.'

'You'll be the star. Business should boom once the rumour gets around we've got us a proper English lady. We can really do with every dollar we make today.'

A silence fell between them, and he wished he'd thought before he spoke. They left his bedroom and walked quietly downstairs.

'Aren't you the glamorous couple?' His mother beamed at them. 'We'll be at the booth by half eleven to give you a break. I've got coffee and blueberry muffins ready in the kitchen for your breakfast.'

'We don't have time to stop.'

'But we'd love some to take with us.' Jenna glanced around at him. 'Wouldn't we?'

'Oh, yeah.' Her thoughtfulness brought back his mom's smile. 'We sure would.'

They left the house with two thermos mugs of coffee and a loaded bag of muffins. While they drove, they chatted and ate.

'You're gonna love the festival. It's a curious combination really. There are people dressed as a variety of Dickens' characters, mainly from *A Christmas Carol* and *Oliver Twist.* John Fraser, one of our family's old friends, has played Fagin for over thirty years now and grows a straggly grey beard specially to play the part. He's originally Scottish but has done a lot of acting in his time so he can nail the Cockney accent. You'll see traditional Victorian era sweets like sugar plums for sale, but they could be next to a vendor selling caramel popcorn – which I'm pretty sure they didn't have in nineteenth-century London.'

Because they were early, he nabbed a spot in the parking garage closest to their booth. All the businesses selling alcohol were gathered in one spot, and no one under twenty-one was allowed to enter that area. When he told Jenna, she looked surprised.

'The Cornish tourist business would suffer a big hit if we had the same licensing laws. Newquay would go bankrupt.' She explained about the seaside town that relied on young surfers and students for the majority of its income. 'Of course, there's a negative side to the way the town's gone downhill, so maybe your idea isn't crazy.' Jenna smoothed down her dress and adjusted her hat before taking his arm.

They swept down the street, then turned the corner to see Tommy waving them over. He had most of the boxes unloaded and stacked up on the ground already.

'There's no sign of young Debbie,' Tommy complained.

'It's early,' Cole said. 'She'll be here.' The set-up took a while, and it was only when they finished he realised his cousin was still missing. 'I'll call Debbie. Don't worry, Tommy. You go off now and we'll see you at one.'

'If you're sure, boss.' Tommy playfully doffed his cap and dodged out of the way of Cole's half-hearted attempt to swipe him.

'What do you want me to do?' Jenna asked.

'Pour out some samples and get ready for the onslaught. Last year, over the two days, the festival attracted more than fifty thousand visitors.' Her eyes widened. 'When we have the long break after our first shift, I'll take you around to see everything. I warn you people will want pictures taken with us. Anyone in costume is considered fair game.' Cole knew he sounded whiney. 'Yeah, I'm a grouch. Maybe they'll nab me to play Scrooge one year.'

'There's nothing mean about you.' Her voice softened.

Before he could respond, his phone buzzed and a message from his uncle popped in. 'Oh great, that's exactly what we don't need. Damn fool girl. I never expected her to pull off this sort of dumb trick.'

'What's she done?'

'Only gone and run away from home last night with Chip Estes. My poor aunt and uncle only found out a few minutes ago when they went to check why she wasn't out of bed and discovered a note she'd left in her bedroom. They've gone to Las Vegas and they're getting married today.'

'You can do that?'

'Yeah, unfortunately. No residency requirement. No waiting period. Pick up a license. Find a wedding chapel and you're all set.' He rattled off the details from memory.

'That's what you did?'

Cole nodded.

'Phone Debbie now.' Jenna sounded insistent. 'Tell her about you and Danielle. It might be enough to stop her going through with it.' She shook her head. 'And don't give me that look.'

'What look?'

'The one that says you wouldn't have listened so why should she?'

He couldn't help smiling. 'How do you know me so damn well in what is it … three weeks?' An adorable blush lit up her skin to clash with her glorious hair. 'If it makes you happy, I'll give it a try.'

'Don't you think her parents will be grateful, even if you fail to persuade her?'

'I guess.' Cole pulled out his phone. 'She'll probably see my name flash up and ignore the call.' After it rang multiple times, he was set to leave a message when Debbie answered. Even the simple 'Hi' she greeted him with sounded defensive.

'I tried to warn y'all I wasn't going to be treated like a child, but you wouldn't listen.'

'If you're getting' married to prove a point, that's dumb.'

Debbie launched into a scathing diatribe and called Cole every name under the sun. 'Let me talk to Jenna.'

He handed the phone over and, after a few minutes of quiet conversation, she persuaded his cousin to give him a second chance, saying there was something he really needed to talk to her about. Debbie's one caveat was that he mustn't say another word against Chip.

'Thanks,' he mouthed. Cole poured out the whole story and his cousin's reaction was instant.

'Shit.'

'Yeah.' He struggled to get it across that if she and Chip were serious about making a life together, it needed to all be done above board. 'Sneakin' around behind the backs of people who love you isn't the right way. I screwed up big time and I don't want you doin' the same. Our folks are gonna be furious when I tell them about me and Danielle, and I don't blame them.'

'I'm not makin' any promises, but I'll think about what you've said and talk it through with Chip.' Her voice wobbled. 'He's not the bad guy y'all think he is. Honestly, he's not.'

For once he sincerely hoped to be proved wrong.

'You can tell Mom and Dad I'm okay and we'll be back soon.'

Jenna whispered that he should make Debbie do that herself. When he lobbed the responsibility back at his cousin it took a few minutes of dead air before she grudgingly agreed.

'I'm real sorry I let you down today.'

'We'll manage.' The lump in his throat tightened. 'You take care, okay?' They'd become much closer since working together and he hated to think of her being hurt. He must have stood there holding the silent phone for a good minute or so before Jenna's gentle voice broke through his thoughts.

'It's almost ten. We need to get back to work.'

'You stopped me being a jerk with Debbie. Thanks.'

‘Any time. But now our first customer is heading this way,’ Jenna warned. ‘Try smiling. You’ll sell more moonshine that way.’

He braced himself and did as he was told.

‘Are you sure Tommy will manage all right? I know your mum and Martin would’ve been happy to stay and help him but they aren’t ... ’ Jenna giggled. ‘I almost said they don’t know a lot about the distillery, then I remembered I’m not exactly an expert either.’

She was starving, her feet were sore and her core temperature might not rise above freezing for a week, but the rush of exhilaration from chatting to the customers and selling more than they’d expected made everything else irrelevant.

‘You’re awesome.’ Cole almost knocked her bonnet off in his enthusiasm to kiss her. ‘Come on. Let’s feed you, then we’ll roam the streets for a while. We should catch the Flat Creek Dancers perform if we’re lucky. There’s a whole bunch of them all in costume and they do something called contra dancing along the main street; it’s a bit like square dancing.’

An hour later, when she’d eaten a roasted turkey leg the size of a small horse, tracked down the sugar plum vendor for some of the sticky sweet treats and listened to a young man playing Christmas carols on water glasses, Jenna totally agreed with Cole’s summing up of the festival. It mashed up historical traditions with up-to-date money-making genius in such a way that the thousands of people swarming around couldn’t be happier.

‘I wish we could pop into more of the shops, but I can’t afford to pay for all the damages we’d incur.’ Navigating the aisles of a small, crowded shop where the shelves were loaded with dangerously expensive ornaments in her extravagant dress had been a frightening experience.

'You can come back another day. All the businesses open extra hours in the run-up to Christmas, and I'm sure they'll be happy to sell you all the festive knick-knacks your heart desires.' Cole looked shame-faced. 'Sorry. I'm spoiling this for you.'

'You're absolutely not.' She couldn't admit that something else was dimming the occasion that no amount of shopping would cure. 'I hear music coming closer to us, and I'm sure it's not the carols all the shops are playing – which, by the way, are nowhere near as original as ours.'

'Nah, of course not.' As their gazes locked, Cole's eyes turned dark. 'I think you're right, though. It's the dancers I was telling you about. Let's go.'

Jenna happily let him cradle his arm around her waist and lead her away. They slipped back into the crowd and spotted the Mother and Father Christmas characters surrounded by visitors having pictures taken with them. Further along, they saw other volunteers dressed up as Tiny Tim and the rest of the Cratchit family; they even met and shook hands with the famous Fagin who made sure one of his urchins 'picked' their pockets.

The music grew louder and they were able to peek through a few gaps between people to watch the dancers, all in costume and swirling to the beat of a fiddler and drummer walking alongside them. Once they finished and moved on down the street, Jenna turned to Cole.

'I'm loving every minute of this—'

'But you're exhausted, right?' Cole squeezed her hand. 'I am, too. Let's go back and we can sit down until it's time to work again.'

As they passed through the security gate, she spotted a large group of Cole's family, including his aunt and uncle, gathered off to one side of their booth.

'Oh great, they've all come to support you.' She didn't understand why Cole looked wary until his mother turned on them with a face like thunder.

'Debbie just phoned her mom and dad. She told them quite an interesting story about why she and Chip are delaying their wedding plans and coming back home. Do you have something important to tell *us* by any chance?' Sylvia promptly burst into tears and Martin tried to comfort her.

'I'm sorry. Really sorry. I tried to tell y'all but …' He stumbled over his words.

'Sorry? You run off and get married to some stranger we've never even heard of and don't even tell your mother!'

Jenna gave Cole a nudge and nodded across at Tommy, who was struggling to cope with a long queue of customers.

'We'll talk about this later. Right now, I've a business to run.'

'Yes, we do.' Jenna linked her arm through his in support and struggled to ignore Mimi's meaningful gaze.

Chapter Nineteen

For Cole, the previous twenty-four hours had resembled wading through quicksand … although cow manure might be a better comparison. He'd put up with everything from his mother's bitter disappointment to ribald jokes from his younger cousins, mostly of the 'What Happens in Vegas stays in Vegas' variety. Jenna had been curiously muted since the news of his brief marriage exploded yesterday and, although he wasn't the most observant man, Cole hadn't missed the glances she exchanged with his grandmother. *What was up with that?*

'I'll see you back at ole Moonshine Holler.' Tommy's grin widened. 'You might want to change out of your fancy clothes first, boss. Can't have you getting' all mucky, can we?'

'Shove off and do your job.' He knew the older man wouldn't take that seriously and they joked around some more before Tommy hopped into the distillery truck and drove off. 'Are you ready to get out of all this gear?' he asked Jenna while tugging off his tie and shoving it in his pocket. 'After we've helped unload, we can have a quiet evening. Don't know about you but I'm bushed.' It clicked that she was staring at the ground instead of him. 'What's up? Have I done somethin' wrong? I know it's been hard work, but I've almost enjoyed doin' all this with you.' Cole grasped her cold hands. 'Talk to me. Look at me.' She raised her head as if it was too heavy to lift, and her bright blue eyes were awash with tears.

'You've done nothing wrong. That's one of the problems.' Jenna's husky voice broke and she tugged her hands out of his grasp. 'Oh Cole, please don't hate me, but there's something I need to say.'

'I could never hate you.' His throat tightened. 'For God's sake, tell me you're not givin' up on us?' The loud clang of metal barriers being stacked up nearby broke into their conversation, and he realised they were in the way of people dismantling the festival equipment. 'Can this wait until we've got the work finished?' Cole sighed. 'I'm not puttin' you off, sweetheart … well, I guess a smidgen of me is but—'

'I understand.'

The worst of it was he knew she absolutely did. He managed to nod and avoided the urge to touch her again. It was a silent drive back to Leiper's Fork, and he was afraid to joke about the new light display he spotted: a curious beach scene with Mary, Joseph and baby Jesus under swaying palm trees, all in bright neon-pink and orange plastic. Jenna's face remained buried in her chest, the epitome of misery. The second they turned into the distillery, she straightened her shoulders and stared at him.

'Do I look okay?'

There were a myriad of ways he could answer the question, but Cole assumed she didn't want Tommy to guess anything was wrong.

He brushed away a smudge of mascara where one rogue tear had sneaked out. 'Beautiful.' A flush of heat tinged her pale skin, but she didn't say a word. Cole jumped out of the truck before he was tempted to say something he shouldn't.

Tommy had the doors to the store room open and the truck backed up to the ramp already. Cole tried to act normal, but when he started to haul out boxes without speaking any more than was necessary, it earned him a few sideways glances. Because they'd sold far more than expected at the festival it didn't take long, and they soon had it all wrapped up. 'Great job.'

'Yeah, we done good.' Tommy grinned at Jenna. 'Keep this up and he might give you a permanent job.'

Her taut smile must have been physically painful to hold in place. For the sake of being kind, he realised he should whisk her out of there as soon as possible, but the longer he delayed leaving put off the moment when he was forced to hear whatever bad news she was saving for him.

‘I’d better get off home.’ Tommy grimaced. ‘I promised Louella we’d pick up the grandkids and take them to that godawful pizza place with the ear-splitting game arcade. It’s payback for me working the festival and leaving her alone all weekend.’

‘How many do you have?’ Jenna asked. Ten minutes later, she knew all about the ten-year-old twin grandsons and five-year-old granddaughter that Tommy doted on. He wondered if she was simply being polite, genuinely wanted to know or was delaying the evil moment. Cole knew which he hoped for. ‘We mustn’t hold you up any longer.’ She exhaled a tiny sigh. ‘I think someone wants to get out of his fancy suit, and I’ll be glad to peel off a few layers.’

A wave of sadness swept through him. Yesterday she’d promised to make him a very happy Victorian gentleman before they got rid of their costumes, but he was pretty sure that wasn’t an option any longer. ‘Yeah, we’ll go as soon as I’ve locked up. Thanks, Tommy.’

‘No problem, boss. Same time next year, eh?’

Cole nodded, not daring to look at Jenna. Who knew what position the distillery would be in by then?

They kept up the civilised pretence until Tommy drove away.

‘We’ll freeze if we stand here talking and your parents will probably be at your house, so why don’t we use your office?’ Jenna swept in through the back door without waiting for an answer, leaving him with no choice but to follow.

The previous night, when she’d laid next to him, soaking up the warmth from his body, the courage to go through with this today almost failed her. But Jenna owed Cole this much at least. In her head she went over and over again how best to approach her confession before deciding it didn’t really matter. Whether she chose the gentle approach and eased around to the subject or ripped the bandage off in one go, it didn't matter. Cole would be heartbroken either way.

Jenna opened the gold-beaded, Victorian-style bag she'd been carrying around for the last two days. 'I've got something to show you.' She passed over her copy of 'Lightning' Landon's letter and watched confusion inch across Cole's face.

'I don't understand. Why did Mimi give you this? Why didn't she just tell me what she discovered about it?'

'Because this isn't the one you found.' Her breathing became laboured. 'It's an identical copy belonging to *my* great grandfather, Jim Richards, better known as "Tucker".'

'*Your* great-grandfather? I don't get it.'

She poured out everything Grandpa Jimmy had told her about his father and Tucker's life in Tennessee. 'Our ancestors were best friends and illegal moonshiners together back in the day.'

'What does the letter say?'

'It's an agreement between the two men and states that the "Lightning Flash" recipe was a collaborative recipe they came up with. Any money they made from selling the moonshine was to be shared equally between them.'

'And that's why you came here?' Cole's voice turned to ice.

Nothing Jenna said now would convince him that she fell in love with him despite who he was and not because of it. She could deny the fact until she was blue in the face, but it wouldn't make any difference.

'Wow, I knew you were clever but you're smarter than I thought.' He shook his head. 'Played us all brilliantly, didn't you? Won over my family … all except for Mimi. You never really fooled her, did you?'

Jenna let the tirade wash over her as the man who'd loved every inch of her the previous night verbally ripped her to shreds. She understood it came from a place of deep, unfathomable hurt, but that didn't make it any easier to endure.

'I'll take you back to the house to collect your things. You'll be hearing from my lawyer. Maybe you and Ralph Bennett can buy me out, because I sure as hell don't want anything to do with the pair of you.' The colour drained from his face. 'Were you in league with him all the time?'

'No! Certainly not.' He didn't look convinced, but then why should he? 'I don't want anything from you. The money never mattered to me, and it still doesn't. I didn't even know if the letter was genuine. My mother always insisted it was a load of rubbish and nothing but the ramblings of a couple of drunks. I only ever wanted to prove the story one way or the other—'

'Don't waste my time and yours dreamin' up excuses because they're not gonna wash.'

'How will you manage the tours and the shop with Debbie gone too?'

Cole's rough laughter turned her stomach. 'Like you care.'

Jenna hadn't only betrayed the deep love they shared, she'd put another nail in the coffin of his precious distillery. For that combination of treachery, he would never forgive her.

'Let's go.' He grabbed his keys off the desk. 'When we get to the house, I'd appreciate it if you avoid saying any more to my folks than absolutely necessary. I'll spin a tale about you needing to leave because of a family emergency back home.' Deep lines creased his face, ageing him before her eyes. 'I'll tell them the truth later when I've calmed down.'

She nodded through a veil of tears. Jenna scraped through the next hour by sheer bloody-minded determination. Mimi had been wrong. The old lady had been certain her grandson would listen reasonably to Jenna's explanation and love her too much to let the news come between them.

Thankfully, Cole wasn't there when she was ready to leave so she didn't have to lie about where she was going. He wouldn't be happy if he'd heard the last thing his grandmother said to her. *'If the boy gets a bit uppity, you come stay with us for a while until he calms down.'*

She'd say his reaction rated a lot higher on the anger scale than 'uppity', but it was dark already and it would be stupid to hurry off to the airport with no ticket booked. Jenna couldn't look in the rear-view mirror as she pulled out of Cole's driveway, leaving him, his love and his beautiful house behind. She held back her tears until she knocked on Eliza's front door. The sight of the Christmas wreath with its jaunty red bow and the waft of cinnamon surrounding Cole's aunt when she came out to greet her broke Jenna's self-control. She couldn't wrap her head around why his family would welcome her but, as she was drawn into a warm hug, that ceased to matter. She'd take any Christmas miracle she was offered and be grateful.

Chapter Twenty

All week Cole struggled to hold things together, but when Saturday evening came around he crashed. On top of his usual work, he'd inexplicably put extra hours into perfecting the special Christmas present he'd dreamed up for Jenna, despite the fact that he'd never give it to her now. The previous evening, when he'd locked the distillery door, everything caught up with him. He should have been starving because he'd barely touched any food since Jenna left, but he was too wiped out to eat. He'd gone straight to bed and slept for thirteen hours straight.

'Betty's cooked your favourite, waffles and bacon.' His mother's voice drifted up the stairs. It had taken him by surprise when their old housekeeper had turned up on Monday morning. According to Sylvia, she declared she didn't want to work for anyone else after all these years. The question of who was going to pay her hadn't arisen yet.

'I'll shower and be down in a few minutes.'

'Oh right. Good.'

He couldn't blame her for sounding surprised, because they'd barely exchanged a dozen words all week. The only positive during the last excruciating seven days came when a rather subdued Debbie turned up on Tuesday morning. His cousin had been her usual forthright self.

'I won't ask you why Jenna isn't here and you look like the Ghost of Christmas Past if you keep your nose out of my private life.'

Cole leaned against the window, pressing his face against the cold glass to stare out at the wintery landscape. The freeze was persisting, very unusual for middle Tennessee, and the weather people were even floating rumours about a possible white Christmas. Not that he cared. He'd be stuck here with his mother and Martin while they all tried to pretend they wouldn't prefer to be elsewhere. The Landon family held their big gathering on Christmas Eve but, with all the problems eating away at him, he wasn't in the mood to face them all.

After the speediest shower on record, he dragged on a chunky black jumper and ragged jeans. Cole reached for his razor and scraped at the thick stubble shadowing his jaw. For two pins he'd crawl back into bed, but he needed to keep his promise and trudged downstairs.

'Good Lord boy, I can see your ribs from here.' Betty scolded him. 'Sit there and get this down you.' She slammed a mammoth plate of food in front of him.

A wash of acid flooded his mouth. 'I'm not hungry, but I'll take some coffee.'

'No you won't. You'll eat every scrap and drink up a big ole glass of orange juice. You haven't had anything decent all week.'

He caught Martin's amusement. 'Yes, ma'am.' After struggling through the first couple of mouthfuls, Cole's appetite kicked back in and he polished off every last bite, almost licking the last traces of maple syrup off the plate. He exhaled a satisfied sigh. 'That was damn good, Miss Betty. Any chance of that coffee now?'

'Just one cup.' She wagged her finger in his face and bustled over to the coffee machine. 'Have you heard from your sweet little English girl?'

Cole turned rigid. Everyone else had tiptoed around him all week, but it was typical that this bluntly spoken older woman had the nerve to speak out.

'Your mother says she's a proper beauty.' Betty held out a steaming mug and he took it, almost in a daze. 'Did you do something to scare her off?'

If his mother hadn't become, for all intents and purposes, estranged from his father's family she would have discovered the truth days ago from Mimi. The anger gnawing at him since Jenna's revelations bubbled back up and he blurted everything out. The three stared at him in shock. 'So there you are. She came here for the specific purpose of claiming half of my business, and our relationship was nothing more than a temporary bonus.'

'You can't believe that for one moment,' Martin murmured. 'We could all see she adored you. Did you actually listen to her explanation or simply blast the poor woman out?' His stepfather held up his hand. 'Oh, you'll say it's no business of mine, but I reckon it is. I've had to tread on eggshells with you for over twenty-five years to keep your mother happy, but I'm tired of it. You've never tried to even meet me half way.' The colour deepened in his face. 'I know I've been a fool and made stupid mistakes, and it galls me like nothing else to have to be grateful to you now.'

Cole stood up. 'Would anyone else like to stick the knife in? Mom? Must be your turn, surely?'

'Oh sweetheart.' Her face was damp with tears. 'I do sympathise. It hurts to find out you've been lied to. She should've been honest from the beginning, but I can see how it spiralled out of control. Maybe Jenna wanted to be honest but the closer the two of you became the more she hated the idea of hurting you?' Sylvia glanced at her husband. 'We know how that is, don't we?'

In a blinding revelation, he recognised their deep love for each other; maybe it'd grown over the years without him being aware of it, but that didn't matter. Cole gulped a few deep breaths before giving Martin a long overdue apology. The man had tried his best to be there for Cole and been swept aside at every turn. 'Any chance we can start over?'

'I'd like that,' Martin said softly. 'I really believe we could have a go at saving those shares in the distillery if we put our brains together.'

'Perhaps.' He didn't want to dash his stepfather's hopes.

'So, are you goin' after your girl?'

'After the way I spoke to her?' Cole shook his head sadly. 'She won't forgive that.'

'But you're willing to forgive the mistakes she made, am I right?' Martin persisted.

'Yeah.'

'Then give her the same opportunity.'

'I'll have to think about it.' By now she was probably four thousand miles away. Even if he wanted to rush off to England he had responsibilities here, and Jenna understood that. She understood everything and loved him anyway. 'I've got some paperwork to do.' Cole forced a tight smile. 'I'm not making that up either. My head's been all over the place this week, and I've fallen way behind.' The smile he gave Betty was more genuine this time around. 'That breakfast should help get my brain in gear.'

'I'm fixing my smothered pork chops tonight with baked sweet potatoes, fried apples and cabbage.'

'You're an angel.' He surprised the housekeeper with a hug. 'Thank you.' She didn't ask him to spell out what for; they both knew he wasn't talking about waffles and bacon.

Jenna tugged her coat in around her and shoved her hands deep in the pockets. This spot in the furthest end of the half-frozen garden was the quietest place she could find away from the busy house. She couldn't believe she was still here. Her intention to leave as soon as she could change her return flight was aborted when she discovered the airline would charge her an exorbitant fee to travel this close to Christmas.

When she told Eliza she couldn't possibly impose on them over the holidays, Cole's aunt told her she was talking nonsense. They were happy to have her stay. Happy wasn't how Jenna would describe her mother's reaction when she emailed to explain her change of plans. The only thing that consoled Anne was that her daughter wouldn't be in Cornwall either. Maybe for her Christmas present she should ask her parents to make an effort to be more amiable with each other. They both had new partners and satisfying lives, so why were they still holding on to all the old anger and putting her slap bang in the middle of it?

In small recompense for the Landons' hospitality, she was trying to make herself useful. Despite her previous dismal failures in the kitchen, she had discovered a surprising talent for baking and there were now thirty miniature cranberry-orange cakes destined as gifts for various friends, dozens of dinner rolls and corn muffins and a massive sour cream chocolate pound cake in Eliza's freezer. She'd already been warned that on Wednesday the pie baking would start in earnest. The Landons held a big family party at lunchtime on Christmas Eve so that their grandchildren could be in their own homes on the day itself and not get dragged away from their presents.

'They're over here again on the twenty-sixth to show off everything they got, and we sort of do it all over again then.' Eliza's explanation came with an indulgent smile.

Cole slipped back into her mind, not that he was ever far away. Certain smells could stop her in her tracks, in particular air-dried clothes and any kind of spices, but they were never him. They'd had no contact since last week's debacle, and no doubt he assumed she'd gone back to England. She couldn't find out any updates from Debbie because the usually chatty girl was unnaturally quiet since she returned. Outside of work, she hung out in her bedroom and avoided her family as much as possible. Chip Estes and what happened in Las Vegas had never been mentioned as far as Jenna knew.

Eliza came bustling out from the house. 'I need my kitchen assistant back at work. We're making cookies for the town carol singing tonight. The local high school choir will be outside Puckett's where we'll have free hot chocolate and cookies set up. The whole family are going, and I reckon you'll enjoy it.'

'I'm happy to help bake, but I can't possibly join you.'

'Because of Cole? It's very unlikely he'll be there; he rarely goes. But you can't keep avoiding him until you get on that plane after New Year.' Eliza's voice softened. 'We're a large, close family. We talk. He's bound to find out you've hung around, even if my Debbie isn't her usual chatty self at work.'

'I'll think about tonight. I promise.'

Six hours later, she sagged into Mimi's old brown recliner and let her eyes close as the front door slammed shut behind Debbie. In the end, no one pestered Jenna again about going to the carol singing and now she was finally alone in the house. Debbie, the last and most reluctant one to leave, was almost dragged out by her father. The poor girl was nothing like her old bubbly self, but Jenna didn't regret encouraging Cole to intervene. Broken hearts were one thing, broken marriages quite another. The rhythmic tick of the old grandfather clock in the corner of the living room soothed her.

She fought hard not to wake up because she didn't want her dream to end. Not only was Cole right beside her, but she could hear his deep, raspy drawl and smell the unique scent that hung around him from the distillery; a smell he'd once poetically described as liquid magic.

'Jenna? Are you tryin' to beat out Sleeping Beauty?'

She opened one eye and almost shot out of the chair. Unless she was going out of her mind, all six-foot-two inches of Cole Landon, grey with exhaustion but still drop-dead gorgeous, was standing close enough to touch. 'What on earth are you doing here? I didn't hear the doorbell and I would, because Mimi made your uncle put up one that plays "God Rest Ye Merry Gentlemen".' She rattled on while wishing her heart rate would settle back to normal.

'Uh, the door's never locked and the family always go in and out as we please.' He looked stern. 'The more pertinent question is what are you doin' here?'

'You didn't know?' Jenna's brief flash of hope died. For a few stupid moments, she thought he'd come on purpose to find her.

'No, I assumed you were back home by now.' He sheepishly brought out a large branch of mistletoe from behind his back. 'My mother sent me over with this. She said Aunt Eliza needed some but …' The ghost of a smile fluttered across his face. 'They didn't drag you to the singin' thing?'

'Your aunt invited me and I said I'd think about it, but Eliza didn't argue later when I said I'd made up my mind not to go.'

'Did you notice her talking with Mimi?'

Jenna struggled to think. 'Yes. I saw them huddled in a corner at one point and then before Eliza came back into the kitchen, I heard her talking to someone on the phone.' She shook her head. 'Your aunt was calling Sylvia, wasn't she?'

'Almost one hundred per cent certain. My family sure are interfering devils.' A rough laugh broke out of him before the frown returned. 'You still haven't said why you're here.'

'Why don't you sit down for a minute? You look wiped out. If you want me to apologise for crashing here with your family on top of everything else, I'm happy to do that.'

Cole muttered something she couldn't make out and dropped down on the sofa, still clutching the mistletoe as if it was a talisman he daren't let go of. For some irrational reason that lifted her spirits. Before he could speak, she quickly explained everything.

'So, my interfering grandmother strikes again? Quite an achievement on Mimi's part to get my mother in on it too. They aren't exactly best buddies.' The sparkling lights from the Christmas tree picked up the freshly washed gleam in his tousled hair when he yanked off his cap.

'Are you mad at them?' She felt an awful lot hung on his answer.

'Mad? No.' Cole's husky whisper tore through her. 'I've been an ass. Even Martin had the nerve to call me out on it.' He sighed. 'I love you for cryin' out loud, and when you tried to explain I wouldn't even listen. What does that say about me?'

Jenna slid down on her knees in front of him. 'I lied. I hurt you. I ruined "us". You had every right to be mad. I should've been up front with you on the day we met.'

'Maybe, but *you* forgave *me* for being married, for God's sake.' He shushed her when she tried to protest. 'Let me own this, okay?' Cole half-smiled when she didn't object. 'I know we've a lot of ground to cover, but I reckon we'll do it better if you're back under my roof.' The brief flash of confidence slipped away. 'I'm takin' too much for granted, aren't I?'

She gestured to the mistletoe. 'If you put that to good use you might have better luck.' It amused her that he was so tired and bewildered it took a few seconds to click.

'Oh, right.' Cole leaned down, held the greenery over their heads and kissed her. Soft as an errant snowflake at first, but as she darted her tongue out to taste him the ice melted. He tossed the mistletoe aside and tugged her up onto his lap.

Jenna moaned as one of his hands slid up under her jumper while the other caressed the back of her neck, twining his fingers through her loose hair.

'I want to do right by you this time around,' he murmured. 'Making love to you here on the sofa and shocking the poor angel on top of the tree would be awesome, but how about we frighten my family instead and turn up at the carol singing?'

'Perfect. We'll save the other awesome for later.' Tears clutched at her throat. Until a few minutes ago, she'd conceded there was no chance of any 'later' for them. Jenna leaned her forehead against his and they stayed that way until he stroked her cheek and whispered that if they didn't move it they would be too late.

They dragged on coats, hats and gloves and jumped into Cole's truck. He gunned the engine and shot off down the road.

'This is the closest we can park.' He flashed a grin and pulled over to stop on the shoulder. 'I'll keep you warm while we walk.'

The crisp air, the twinkling lights decorating the shops they passed, the noisy good-natured crowd and 'Hark the Herald Angels Sing' blasting out of the loudspeakers all added to their good spirits.

'We'll try to get near to Puckett's and keep our eyes open for the Landon mob.' Almost before the words left his mouth, a shrill whistle rose pierced the general clamour. 'That's Mimi.'

'What is?'

'The whistle.' He craned his neck. 'There they are. In front of the coffee shop.' Cole lifted one hand to wave. 'Should we pretend to be mad at her?'

'Don't be daft. She's not stupid.' Jenna linked her arm through his. She didn't want to fool anyone any longer.

Chapter Twenty-One

Cole knew he'd surprised Tommy and the rest of the guys this morning when he'd arrived later than usual and strolled into the distillery hand in hand with Jenna whistling 'Rudolph the Red Nosed Reindeer'. A few eyebrows raised when he announced she would be leading tours and working in the store again, but that was it. The gloves would be off when they had their customary staff party after they closed the doors on Thursday for their four-day Christmas break. Tongues always loosened after a few shots of Lightning Flash.

Through his open office door, he spotted Debbie slumped with her elbows on the bar. Luckily, Ashley was manning the till but a queue was forming in front of her, so Cole pushed his chair back and headed out to help. His cousin straightened up when she saw him coming but he motioned her to stay put; Jenna's tour would finish in a few minutes, and Debbie would be on tasting duty then. It was non-stop for a while until they were finally able to take a breather.

'Have you been at the Mistletoe Madness?' Ashley laughed at him. 'I've never seen you so jovial.' She nodded across the room at Jenna who had brought her group out and was giving them the usual spiel before handing them over to his cousin. 'I suspect a certain lady has somethin' to do with your good mood.'

'Yeah, you hit the nail on the head.' *No point denying it.* For once he'd relaxed and enjoyed chatting to the customers. Jenna was right; a different mind-set did the trick. He was the face of Landon Hollow and needed to step up more. The shop sales combined with the tours were a huge chunk of his business, and he needed to give them more attention. 'You got big plans for Christmas?'

'The usual … oh Lord, Cole. Here comes trouble.'

He glanced over and saw Chip Estes heading straight for his cousin.

‘What are you doin’ here?’ Debbie was red-faced and furious. ‘Clear off. I told you we’re through.’

Why did everyone treat his distillery as the go-to place to hold their arguments? ‘I’ll sort it.’ Cole hurried across and greeted Chip like a long-lost friend, whisking the confused young man away to his office before he knew what hit him. Over his shoulder, he saw Jenna hand Debbie a bottle and encourage her to pour out more samples for the tour group. ‘Sit down.’ He gave Chip a slight shove into a chair. ‘Now, I don’t know what’s goin’ on between you and my cousin, but I’ve got a business to run and y’all aren’t helping.’ Out of nowhere the man dropped his head in his hands and broke down crying; noisy, gulping sobs that frightened the life out of Cole. ‘You’re not teetotal are you?’

Chip wiped at his eyes and blew his nose. ‘No. Why?’

From his private stash, Cole poured a couple of generous shots of Lightning Flash and pushed one across the desk. ‘I reckon a little of my ancestor’s therapy might help.’ A sliver of humour brightened his visitor’s blotchy face. ‘If you want to talk, feel free. If not, you’d better drink up and leave. I’m not having my cousin upset or my business disrupted.’

‘Sorry.’ Chip drained his glass and the moonshine did its work. The whole story tumbled out, starting with the secretive relationship they began six months ago all the way up to the half-assed plan to elope. Debbie had dreamed that up when she became convinced her family would never welcome Chip. Cole couldn’t help wincing as he’d been one of the doubters when he first found out the couple were dating. ‘She told me everything you said when you called her in Las Vegas, and I suggested we returned to Tennessee right away. I reckoned we needed to be honest and up front with our families and take things slower. They need to see I’m not a teenage hot-head any longer. I’m goin’ back to school. I wanna train to be a paramedic.’ Chip shoved a hand through his straggly, dark hair. ‘Took it the wrong way, didn't she? Thought I was tryin' to break up with her. I've been calling and texting non-stop, but she's blocked me.'

Something had to be done. Maybe it was time to channel some of his grandmother's interfering nature. Debbie was obviously unhappy and so was this guy, who seemed genuinely in love with his cousin. 'Stay there. I'll go talk to her and see what I can do.' Cole pointed to the mistletoe hanging over his desk, courtesy of Jenna. 'Remember, that's there for a reason.'

'She'll crush the berries and poison me with them.'

'Have faith. It's Christmas.' A little of that same optimism sneaked into him too. Maybe things could turn around for the distillery, but if they didn't Jenna still loved him and he was closer to his parents than he'd been in years. Things weren't all bad.

Jenna loved her wonderful man, but when she picked up on Chip's distress in the seconds before Cole slammed the office door shut, her heart sunk. Deep, emotional conversations weren't his thing.

'What do you think they're saying?' Debbie whispered.

'You're going to find out.' Her heart fluttered as it did every single time she saw Cole. Maybe one day she'd take the sight of him for granted, but that wouldn't be any time soon. Debbie calmed down a few notches by the end of the tasting session and they talked things through quietly. Her friend conceded she might have been rash to push Chip away, but now pride held her back from admitting that to the man in question.

'Hi Debs.' Cole blocked his cousin's attempt to avoid him. 'Hear me out a minute. That's all I'm askin'. The guy in there loves you, and I reckon I misjudged him. We should've given you more credit too. You wouldn't have fallen for Chip if he hadn't grown up. Go talk to the poor devil, please,' he begged.

'You're miserable and he's clearly miserable too.' Jenna caught Cole's eye. 'Saying sorry is hard. Being honest is hard. But the rewards … they're well worth it.'

'They sure are.' Cole grinned and popped a quick kiss on her mouth.

'Fine.' Debbie snorted and stalked off.

'Think we've done the right thing?' he muttered. 'I didn't have a clue what I was doin' in there.'

'I bet you plied him with moonshine.' She noticed that he couldn't help but smirk. 'Don't worry, I considered it too but was afraid my boss would catch us drinking on the job.'

'Yeah, we all know what a hard taskmaster he is.' Cole's flagrant wink made her giggle. 'He's hopin' you'll come Christmas shopping with him after work, and then he's gonna cook dinner for you.'

'And for dessert?'

His searing gaze dragged over her. 'That would be you.' He covertly gave her a squeeze. 'I've got shelves to stock and you've got the tasting to clear up. See you at five o'clock.'

'Do you think Debbie and Chip will be all right?'

'My office door's still closed, and we haven't heard anyone yelling or the sound of glass breaking.' Cole grimaced. 'Of course I might have to disinfect my desk later.'

'Your desk … mmm, I hadn't considered that.'

His jaw dropped.

'Off you go.' Jenna gave him a gentle push and returned to work with a broad smile on her face.

Cole would never look at his office in quite the same way again and the woman snuggled up next to him in bed was totally to blame. Well, not totally he supposed. These things took two. Last night their satisfaction at bringing Debbie and Chip back together again had spilled over after the distillery doors were locked and the rest of the staff left. When he told her the shops would stay open until at least seven and asked how much shopping time she needed, Jenna gave him a teasing smirk.

'Why? Is there something you want to do first?'

He'd slowly unfastened the tiny red buttons on the silky blouse she'd changed into. 'Yeah. You.' At that point he swept everything off his desk and settled her on the edge. 'Do we need mistletoe?' Her answer came in the form of reaching for his belt buckle. It briefly flitted through his head to wonder what 'Lightning' Landon would think, but as long as they weren't sullying Bubbling Bertha, he guessed his ancestor would turn a blind eye.

When they'd finally reached the shops, Jenna had impressed him with her decisive gift-choosing skills – she'd been as eager as him to hurry back to Landon House. Cole had managed to suppress a smile when she fretted over whether his mother would like the scarf she'd selected for Sylvia.

'She's got such good taste, I'm not sure—'

'It's perfect.' Cole gathered her back into his arms. 'Like you.' That comment made her eyes darken.

'We both know that's not true.'

They'd talked well into the night and watched the sunrise together. She balked when he promised that the distillery's lawyer would look into the letters they'd found. Fair was fair. He refused to build Landon Hollow's success on the back of a lie.

'I'm gonna call my attorney first thing when we get to work. He won't do much until after the holidays, but it'll get the ball rolling.'

'I wish you wouldn't.'

'We're not arguing about this, honey. I want everythin' above board between us.' Cole kissed the frown lines creasing her forehead, but they didn't go away. 'I thought we were good?'

‘We are.’ Jenna’s voice wobbled. ‘You’ve been incredibly patient and not pressed to hear more about my family, but I want to get it out of the way.’

It struck him as a strange expression to use but he let her continue.

‘Mum left us when I was about fifteen. She was fed up not having a life outside of The Green Parrot, but Dad couldn’t understand that because the pub means everything to him. Then Fred Warren came along; he worked for the beer glass supplier, and they had an affair. He persuaded her to move to Watford with him and she pleaded with me to go with her, but I’d grown up in St. Minack and didn’t want to leave my friends and school ... everything I knew.’

‘It would’ve been tough.’

‘Dad paid off Mum to stop her claiming a share of the pub.’ Her cheeks heated. ‘As much as anything, that’s what makes me frightened of what any claim I have on the distillery could do to you. To us.’

‘It’s totally different. They’d fallen out of love. We’ve fallen into it. I promise we can work this out.’ Cole’s stomach contracted. That wasn’t a lie, but with Ralph Bennett factored in the truth wasn’t straightforward either. ‘So, things are still strained between them?’

She snorted. ‘Strained? That’s putting it mildly. It’s ridiculous. Mum’s happily remarried and Dad is too now, but they still make snide jibes at each other all the time through me. I suppose I just wish they’d … grow up.’ Jenna nodded.

‘Have you told them how it makes you feel?’

‘Not in so many words.’

‘Maybe you should.’ Cole hurried to backtrack. ‘Hey, I’ve no right to give you advice. Until recently Mom and I rarely talked about my dad’s death. My relationship with Martin is a whole other can of worms. At least we’re working on it now, so that’s an improvement. That doesn’t cover the rest of my family who don't know anythin' about the mess we're in at the distillery.'

'Tell them. I'll help you.'

'Thanks, but I don't want to wreck Christmas.' Cole brushed a lock of hair from her face. 'It's the first one I've looked forward to since I was a kid.'

'Me too.'

'But?'

'You're under a time crunch. New Year will be here before you know it, and if you got it out of the way …' Jenna's voice trailed away.

'I'll think about it.' The damn clever woman often planted an idea for him to stew over at his own pace. 'Right now I'm gonna make love to you again, and then it's off to work for us.'

'Oh, really?'

'Yeah, really.' Cole put his hand on her soft breast. 'If that's okay with you?'

Jenna's husky laughter broke free. 'Come here, you silly man.'

With her sapphire eyes sparkling at him and her elegant hands reaching out for him, Cole felt that Christmas really had come early this year.

Chapter Twenty-Two

Jenna spotted Sylvia trotting around the distillery with her watering can and made a swift decision to take the plunge. Hopefully after a few Christmas Eve drinks with the rest of the staff, Cole would be mellow enough to take her interference the way it was meant: out of an abundance of love for him.

She smoothed down her hair and straightened her shirt collar. Simply being within a ten-mile radius of Sylvia Landon Buchanan made her feel scruffy.

'May I have a quick word?' Jenna nabbed the other woman by the T-shirt display. 'I want to ask you a huge favour … it's for Cole really.'

'Of course.'

By the time she'd finished explaining her idea, Sylvia was frowning.

'You want Martin and I to go to Adam and Eliza's party early, humiliate ourselves by admitting to all our money problems and plead for their help?'

If Jenna had asked her to run through Leiper's Fork naked except for a pair of plastic reindeer antlers, Sylvia couldn't sound more appalled. Her brief flash of sympathy dissipated when she recalled Cole's struggle to keep everything together. 'It's going to come out one way or another. Your son will be forced to tell them if you don't. Do you honestly think that's fair?'

'You aren't as "nice" as you appear, are you?' A hint of admiration lurked behind the sharp retort. 'I'll raise the subject with Martin.'

'Will you let me know if you're going to follow through?"

'Forewarned is forearmed?'

'Absolutely.' Jenna spotted Cole coming out of his office and heading straight for them.

'Where are my mistletoe girls?' He grinned and swung his arms around their shoulders.

'Have you been drinking?' Sylvia pulled away, tutting at a splash of water that'd dripped onto her red silk suit.

'Nah, but apart from a few minor blips, life is pretty damn good. Best Christmas ever.'

She caught his mother's dismay. Sylvia might not call losing her beautiful house, most of her money and being obliged to move in with her adult son a minor blip.

'Heck, sorry Mom.' Cole's face crumpled. 'Mr Tactless, that's me.'

'It's all right, sweetheart. It's wonderful to see you happy.' Sylvia swallowed hard. 'Passion for your work is a wonderful thing, but there's got to be more to life and you've re-discovered that with this wonderful young lady.' She patted Jenna's arm. 'I'm leaving now. Will we be seeing you both at Adam and Eliza's tonight?'

'You're going?' He looked extremely surprised.

'Yes, Martin and I thought it was time we made a friendly overture.' A tinge of colour popped into her hollow cheeks. 'Long past time, to be honest.'

'Awesome.' He beamed at Jenna. 'We've got the staff party here first, but it won't run very late because everyone's got family things to get home to. We should be there by around sevenish.' Cole glanced towards the shop. 'Ashley's snowed under. I'll go give her a hand.'

'And I've got another tour starting soon.' Jenna smiled back at him. 'My last one until after the big day.'

'There's no rest when your boss is such an ogre.' If his eyes twinkled any more they'd outshine the Christmas tree. 'See you later, Mom.'

After he hurried off, Sylvia grasped her arm.

'We'll do it.'

'Are you sure it'll be okay with Martin?'

Sylvia's expression hardened. 'If he wants to stay married, it will be.'

'You're not so "nice" yourself, are you?' Jenna chuckled. 'I like that.'

'Cole better not mess things up with you or he'll have me to answer to.'

If she'd stepped over some invisible line by arranging this, it could wreck everything.

He wouldn't call himself a religious man, but Cole glanced surreptitiously at the eight of them, grouped in a semi-circle of chairs around Bubbling Bertha, and said a fervent prayer to whomever might be listening that he could find a way to save this. It wasn't simply the end product – although that was important – but these people were family too.

They'd demolished the pizzas he'd had delivered and the moonshine had been flowing since they locked up at five o'clock after the last visitors. Nobody had driven in this morning and he had ride-share cars organised that would arrive in about another ten minutes to take them all home safely. Jenna's drowsy head rested on his shoulder. She'd probably indulged in a little too much Mistletoe Madness.

'Y'all help yourselves to a bottle of whatever you like on the way out. No wrapping required. My kind of gift.' Cole cleared his throat. 'I'm not gonna get all misty-eyed over you bunch of reprobates, but you know how I feel about y'all. There wouldn't be a Landon Hollow Distillery without your hard work. Enjoy the holiday with your families and I'll see you Tuesday morning, bright and early.'

'If your drawl gets much thicker we could use it for wallpaper paste,' Jenna whispered in his ear. 'Another shot of Cinnamon Fire and I'm not going to understand a single word you say. Wrap it up and let's get going.'

'Keen to get me to yourself, are you?' He plastered a hot, heavy kiss on her mouth and raucous cheers broke out, along with several comments he hoped she couldn't translate.

'We've another party to go to, in case you'd forgotten.' A shadow briefly darkened her eyes and he wondered what that was about. He struggled to his feet, pulling her with him. 'Debbie, you gonna ride with us?'

'No. Chip's parked outside waiting for me. We're goin' together.' A wry smile creased her face. 'Making him brave the lion's den on his own wouldn't be kind.'

'Sure wouldn't.' Cole clasped her shoulder. 'Tell the poor guy there'll be plenty of food so we won't need to eat him.'

'I can vouch for that.' Jenna chimed in. 'We baked non-stop last week.'

The party started to break up and soon they were the last ones left.

'I don't suppose we've got time to … check out my desk again?' Her rich, spicy scent, the hints of vanilla and lime drifting up from her silky hair and the haze provided by the moonshine all conspired to make him ache for this amazing woman.

'No, Mr Landon. Definitely not.' Her gaze turned to molten glass. 'You'll have to hold the thought and everything else until later. If you've been a good boy, Father Christmas might bring you something extra special this year.'

'He already did.' Cole's voice turned raspy. 'Let's get out of here before I lose the will to spend the evening being crawled over by over-excited kids and listening to Uncle Adam's ancient Johnny Cash and Willie Nelson Christmas albums.'

'You love it really.'

Denying it would be pointless and, since Jenna had come into his life, the value of what he already had seemed more vivid. 'Come on, let's kick off Christmas.'

'So that's how things are, and I hope you'll help the poor guy out.'

Jenna's heart leapt in her throat as she heard Martin's booming voice when they walked through Adam Landon's front door.

'What's he on about now?' Cole was loose-limbed and smiley, and she hated to see his good mood spoiled. 'I'm tryin' to be more tolerant, but the guy still bores me to death.'

She stuck with a commiserating shrug. This could be one of her worst ideas ever.

'Come on, let's join the party.' His arm tightened around her waist and Cole steered her towards the family room where everyone was gathered. 'Here we are. We come bearing presents.' He swung a loaded bag in one hand and the smaller kids swarmed around them.

Apparently it was tradition to let the younger family members go ahead and open their gifts from people they wouldn't see on Christmas Day. She relaxed her wariness for a few minutes amid the chaos of ripped paper and excited shrieks. It wasn't hard to get in the festive spirit as bubbly little Abigail, Danny's daughter, almost exploded with joy when she discovered the Peppa Pig camping set she'd been begging for.

'You shouldn't have spent as much on the kids this year.' Adam told Cole off.

'Why ever not? That's what uncles are for. You always spoiled me. Remember the remote control police car? Mom and Dad told you off but you told them to pack sand – not in so many words maybe, but that's what you meant.'

'That's different. I could afford it.' Adam frowned. 'Why didn't you tell us the distillery was in trouble?'

'Is that what you were talking about when I came in? Where did you hear that?' Cole asked. He turned and shot Jenna a fierce glance. 'You knew about this?'

Before she could figure out how to reply, his mother dropped her right in it.

'She suggested that we—'

'Came here beggin' for help?' Cole sounded disgusted. 'I'm goin' outside.' He threw off her hand. 'If I stay, I'll say somethin' the kids don't need to hear.' He threw open the French doors leading to the back garden and let in a blast of cold air.

She was torn between following him and attempting to sort out the upset he'd left behind.

'There's hot cider and a bunch of desserts in the kitchen,' Eliza announced. 'Debbie, could you and Chip see to things while we chat a bit?'

'Sure, Mom.' Debbie dragged her startled boyfriend away. Jenna felt for him because she remembered being overwhelmed by the Landon clan at Thanksgiving.

'Maybe tonight wasn't the best time, but it's done now so let's work out how to bring the boy around.' Eliza spoke up first.

'It's all my fault.' Jenna sighed. 'I encouraged Sylvia and Martin to tell you everything. After all my lies and dishonesty I thought it was for the best, but I didn't take Cole's feelings into account enough.'

'I'll go talk to the boy,' Mimi said. 'We've hurt his pride.'

'Thank you.'

Eliza fetched her mother-in-law a warm coat and scarf before she let her anywhere near the door. 'As sure as God made green apples, we're in for snow tonight. I don't need you catching a chill and getting sick.'

An awkward silence swallowed them up and Jenna hovered on the edge of tears. The monogrammed red and green Christmas stockings hanging from the brick fireplace, the piles of colourfully wrapped presents stacked under the tree and low hum of carols playing in the background didn't help her mood. *So much for this being the best Christmas ever*. She should have let him come around to things in his own way instead of forging thoughtlessly ahead.

Voices drifted in through the door; Cole's louder and occasionally raised, but his grandmother's remaining calm and persuasive.

'Should we leave?' Sylvia sounded worried. 'We didn't mean to spoil the party, but I really wanted to mend the fences between us and this seemed the ideal way. Bring us all together. Be the family that we should be.' Her voice cracked. 'Trey did his best, but I never quite fitted in.'

'That wasn't only your fault,' Eliza admitted. 'We didn't make you as welcome as we should've done.' She gave a tiny smile. 'You made me feel … country. You're always so well-dressed and polished.'

'It's simply the way my mother taught me to be. I envied you being so comfortable in yourself. Your big family. How close you all were … are. That put a barrier between myself and Trey which shouldn't have been there.'

'I haven't helped either.' Martin looked shamefaced. 'I was too full of fancy ideas and I resented Trey. Competing against someone who died a tragic death far too young was tough on my ego.'

'You never needed to compete.'

'I realise that now.' Martin slumped on the sofa next to his wife. 'I've screwed up everything.'

'No you haven't.' Cole strode back in with his smiling grandmother by his side. 'It took guts to come here today and spill the beans.' He flashed Jenna a grateful look. 'You had guts, too. More than me.'

The knot in her stomach loosened.

'If y'all are still willing to help, I'm happy to talk about it.' Cole huffed out a weary sigh. 'I'm a loner by nature, or by circumstance, not sure which, but it's dumb and you're my tribe, same as the distillery workers are. I should've told everyone straight out what was goin' on and asked for advice and ideas.' He struggled to smile. 'I reckon together we can beat Ralph Bennett any day.'

'Amen to that.' Mimi's loud agreement made everyone smile. 'My old bones are cold, so I'm gonna sit by the fire and this boy can bring me a hot chocolate with plenty of marshmallows and a slice of the chocolate cake our Jenna whipped up. There's no such thing as too much chocolate at Christmas.'

Our Jenna. She loved the sound of that. Christmas miracles came in all shapes and sizes and theirs had arrived in the form of his smart, kind grandmother.

'Let's hear Merle Haggard and "The Little Drummer Boy", Adam.' Mimi kicked off her shoes and stretched out her swollen ankles. 'Get all the kiddies back in here. They're what Christmas is about.'

Cole perched on the arm of her chair and pressed a kiss on Jenna's head. 'Sorry I was an ass.'

'We both were. We'll compare notes later.' Her hushed promise made him blush. 'A few hours and you get to open your stocking.'

'Did I hear the word stocking? I hope that's in the plural.'

'Wait and see.' Jenna snuggled into his shoulder and sighed. Contentment was a strange thing; often a person didn't recognise it in the moment, but today she absolutely did and was determined to savour every moment. For now, she refused to think about the return date on her plane ticket.

Chapter Twenty-Three

'Come back to bed, you'll get cold.' Cole's raspy voice stirred her.

'You can come over here instead and warm me up. It's too beautiful to miss.' Jenna stared at the thick blanket of snow disguising everything except the distillery roof, still visible through the trees.

'So are you.' He padded across the floorboards and tightened his large, capable hands around her waist, nestling Jenna back against his bare skin. 'Fancy making a snowman?'

'That is *so* not what I expected you to ask.' She wriggled around to face him and laughed at his fake-offended expression.

'My mind isn't always on sex.'

'Uh, it wasn't your mind that was making itself known shall we say.' With a small shift of her hips she made him groan. 'Happy Christmas.'

'It sure is.' A wickedness sneaked into his gleaming silver eyes, seconds before he swept her off her feet and deposited her in the middle of his crumpled bed. 'Time to make it even happier I reckon.' With his typical thoroughness, no inch of Jenna's tingling body went untouched until she was begging for more. 'By the way, what happened to the stockings I was promised?'

'You want to stop now?'

'I don't consider it stopping.' Cole's lazy smile matched his teasing drawl. 'Call it raising the stakes.' He rolled off her, rested his hands behind his head and winked. 'Make me beg.'

Five minutes later, he did.

Jenna tended to be practical when it came to her underwear but everything was different with Cole. It helped that, apart from the one reference to a corset, he'd never brought up the subject so when she discovered the set of sinful red lace in one of Franklin's exclusive boutiques, it seemed churlish to leave it there. That combination, along with fine black silk stockings that elongated and slimmed her legs, reduced him to jelly.

'You're lovin' this.' He reached up to touch her. 'I am too. Come here.'

This time she didn't protest and it took a while – a long, wonderful while – before they collapsed exhausted, their limbs tangled in the sheets and each other.

'Are you gonna call your folks to wish them Merry Christmas?'

'I suppose so.'

Cole propped up on one elbow. 'Want a suggestion?

'Okay.'

'Feel free to tell me to mind my own business, but you could call your mom and dad on a video chat together. Tell them what you really want for Christmas.' He smoothed a hand over her mussed up hair.

'It *is* your business. I'll do it, but I need you there with me. It'll bolster my courage and I'd really like you to meet them ... virtually at least.'

'Be happy to.'

'But?' She'd picked up an almost imperceptible hesitance.

'It's nothing to do with calling your folks, but you've got a ticket back home a week on Monday, right?'

Those few words leeched the colour from the day.

'We've gotta face it and decide what we're gonna do.'

'I know,' she whispered. 'But not today.'

'Sorry.' Cole brushed a kiss over her mouth. 'You're right. Let's not spoil Christmas.' The smile didn't quite reach his eyes. 'When's a good time to call?'

'Dad closes the Parrot mid-afternoon for a couple of hours before he opens again for the evening. Mum and Fred are on their own so it shouldn't matter much to them. If we call just after nine here, that'll work.'

'I was thinking of cooking breakfast for us all first.'

The thought of eating made her stomach clench.

'Hey, I'm not a complete insensitive jerk, you know,' he murmured. 'Doesn't help we've got my folks here. I know Mom can be a bit rigid … it's the way she was brought up.'

'But you love her anyway, and that's how it should be.' She stopped there because he didn't need all her insecurities dumped on him.

'She's never goin' to be like Aunt Eliza. Doesn't mean she thinks any less of you. It's simply her way.'

Jenna watched him drag on a pair of sweatpants and a baggy dark blue jumper.

'We'll shower later.'

'We will?'

'Yeah. We can swap our presents then. In private. There's no big dinner to fix.'

The four of them had agreed that, with Betty taking a few days off over the holidays, they were happy to forego a traditional Christmas dinner. Their plan was to make a meal out of their favourite appetisers later in the day whenever it suited them.

'You think I've got you something else?'

He dragged her close and nuzzled kisses on her neck, and lower. 'Tie a big red bow around you and I'll be a happy man.'

'Cheap. I like that.' Jenna wriggled away. 'I suggest you go and get breakfast going while I dress. If I sit across from your glamorous mother looking like this I might as well plaster a sign across my forehead that says "ravished all night".'

'You've forgotten this morning.'

A rush of heat zoomed up her neck. 'I certainly haven't.' That would stick in her memory for a long time. When she was seventy, would this amazing time in Tennessee be simply a blip in the roadmap of her life, or something to share with this special man as they recalled their early days together?

Cole cradled her face in his warm, sure hands. 'We'll remember it together. Always.' She clung to him, desperate to believe.

While he loaded the dishwasher, Cole listened to the conversation going on behind him as Jenna and his parents swapped Christmas memories. If anyone had asked him a couple of months ago how he envisioned the holiday season, he would have said that he'd be immersed in work until the last minute. After a brief appearance on Christmas Eve at the Landon family party, he would have eaten a duty Christmas Day lunch at his mother's Belle Meade house and then plunged straight back into work. Instead, everything had been turned upside down thanks to the laughing redhead coaxing Martin to tell her about the Christmas he'd split his knee open trying to ride his first bicycle, left by Santa, while his parents were still asleep.

'They didn't know I was out of bed, let alone outside on the sidewalk. At least hospital emergency rooms are pretty damn quiet at five o'clock on Christmas morning.' Martin chuckled.

He noticed her glance at her watch. 'We're goin' to call Jenna's folks in a minute. Do you mind clearing up breakfast, Mom?'

'We'll be happy to. Please wish them Merry Christmas from us my dear and I hope …' Sylvia turned pink. He guessed she almost said something on the lines of hoping to meet them, before considering it might be inappropriate so soon. Telling her they'd passed inappropriate weeks ago wouldn't be wise.

They headed upstairs where it would be quieter to talk. 'How're you goin' to play this?'

'I think I'll get Mum on first then try to bring Dad in too before she can object.' She huffed out a heavy breath. 'Wing it from there, I suppose.'

They settled on the loveseat in his bedroom and he slid his arm behind her shoulder.

'Hello, Mum. Happy Christmas.' Jenna had angled the phone so Anne couldn't see him yet. 'Do you mind hanging on a minute while I fetch something?' She tapped the phone and waited for her father to respond.

'Hello, my 'andsome. I hoped you'd have a minute to fit in a call to your old dad.'

Jenna switched the call to encompass the three of them, and there were a couple of loud gasps from Anne and a 'bloody hell' from Harry Pendean.

'You both asked me what I wanted for Christmas … well, this is it.'

Cole's pride in her swelled as she calmly explained how the way they'd been behaving for the last two decades made her feel. 'I understand you couldn't live together any longer, but you're both happy with your new lives now, so can't you let go of the past?'

The silence stretched out so long that he wondered if they'd lost the connection.

'Before you say anything, there's someone here with me I want you to meet.' Jenna turned the phone to include them both while she introduced him.

Video calls always made him awkward and tongue-tied; not the impression he wanted to portray today.

'I've a lot to tell you both, but I'll ring again in a few days for a proper chat.' She threw him a smile. 'When we've sorted a few more things.'

Thank goodness she had her wits about her because all he'd done was mumble a few Christmas greetings and smile like a demented Cheshire cat. When Jenna hesitated, he shook his brain back into gear. 'I hope I'm not talkin' out of place here … but how do you feel about your daughter's wish? Is it really too much for her to ask? You don't have to be best buddies but the two of you are her parents and you both obviously love her.'

'It's not too much at all … in fact, it's probably too little.' Harry shook his head. 'I'm sorry Jenna, sorrier than I can say.' His face flushed. 'I owe you an apology too, Anne. I was some bitter when you went off and it became a habit.' Next thing, a smiling, grey-haired woman shifted in to share the screen with him. 'My Wendy here is always telling me off.'

'Fred does the same to me,' Anne admitted. 'Come here, Fred.' Now they could see the bald, embarrassed looking man sitting by her. 'I'm sorry, Jenna – and to you too, Harry.'

Cole saw the tears brimming out over Jenna's eyes. This meant everything to her. 'We'd better go now and leave you to the rest of your Christmas Day. Hopefully I'll meet you both in person before too long.' He hadn't intended to say that, and Jenna looked stunned. In the rush of goodbyes he hoped no one noticed that he was the one doing all the talking. 'I'd say that went pretty good.' Cole studied her. 'I spoke out of turn, didn't I?' He slowly stood. 'I'm going to shower. Then I guess we'll have "The Talk" we've been putting off.' While he moved around, found clean clothes and then headed for the bathroom, she had ample opportunity to stop him. Her silence killed him.

When Cole stated his intentions it sent a wave of panic coursing through her which was ridiculous, because she had planned to bring up the subject of visiting England together soon herself. Was she so insecure that having the initiative taken away freaked her out?

She peeled off her clothes. 'Is there room for one more?' The question was rhetorical because his shower was the largest she'd ever seen. He'd once admitted that it was his biggest indulgence when he renovated the house. 'I'm talking about room for one very apologetic redhead, in particular.'

Cole pushed open the glass door. 'Only if she lets this idiot apologise first.'

'Let's do it together.' Jenna stepped in, wrapped her arms around his neck and drew him down for a wet, steamy kiss.

They were almost waterlogged by the time they turned the water off.

'I hope your mom and Martin don't need a bath any time soon.' She grabbed a warm towel from the heated rail. 'In case I didn't make myself clear enough, I'd love for us to go to England together.'

'Oh, I got the message.' Cole's eyes shone. 'Next week won't work for me, though. I've got to sort out the distillery problems first … what I really mean is *we* need to crack it, because I can't manage it without your help.'

'You have it.' Jenna grabbed hold of his hands. 'Now and always … if that's what you want?'

'If? I sure do.' His intense stare reduced her to jelly. 'Is it time for more presents now?'

'It might not be a bad idea if we get dressed first.'

'You've never done a naked gift swap before?'

'Is that a Tennessee tradition?'

He grinned like a mischievous little boy. 'It's a new one I'm starting today.' Cole grabbed a couple of small paper cups from beside the sink and led her back into the bedroom. 'I don't have any proper glasses up here so we'll have to improvise.'

'What are we drinking?'

'One of your Christmas presents.' He dived into his closet and pulled out a red gift bag. 'I hope you like it.'

Jenna got rid of the gold tissue paper and pulled out a large glass bottle. Her skin tingled as she read the words on the distinctive dark green and gold Landon Hollow label. 'Cornish Maid.'

'You said y'all eat strawberries and cream with some sort of biscuity things – scones, wasn't it? – so I tried to capture that flavour combo. I hope I've got the balance right. You'll have to thank Tommy too, because I had to let him in on the secret and ask for his help. He's the real distillery genius. We ran the smallest batch possible but there's plenty more where this came from.' His ears turned pink. 'I did a spot of research on Cornwall and found that maid was an affectionate term y'all use.'

'It is.' Her throat tightened. In the middle of everything, this wonderful man had taken the time to create something unique for her. 'You know this will be a hard act to follow next Christmas.'

'Oh, I've got a few ideas.'

'I'm sure you do.' She appreciated his reticence. Once before he'd rushed into something and lived to regret it. Jenna didn't intend to be another mistake. 'Are you going to pour us a drink?' It was both amusing and touching to watch his obvious nerves when she took her first sip. 'Oh my goodness, that's divine. How did you capture the creaminess so perfectly?'

'I used pure Madagascar vanilla.'

'It's so fruity and smooth.'

'Nothing like most people's perceptions of moonshine.' Cole grinned. 'Perceptions are funny things, aren't they? A bit like relationships.'

'I propose a toast to us.' She raised her paper cup in the air. 'To Cornish Maid and Cinnamon Fire. I'd say we're the perfect blend for a perfect Christmas.'

Chapter Twenty-Four

'Mom, for heaven's sake, sit down and relax. Please. It's only family coming over,' Cole begged. His mother had been scuttling around like a chicken with its head cut off since early this morning. When his aunt suggested they got together the day after Christmas to try to figure out how to keep the distillery in the family, he'd recklessly suggested they met at his house.

'Are you sure? It'll be the whole crowd, kids and all.'

A slightly leaden feeling lodged in his stomach when Eliza questioned him. He certainly never intended to make his family feel unwelcome but hadn't gone out of his way to do the opposite either. Finally, he convinced his aunt that he meant what he said.

He followed the fragrant, spicy scent drifting out from the kitchen. 'Mm, they look good.' Cole snatched a miniature pie from one of the wire racks and took a bite.

'Careful, they're—'

'Hot.' He juggled it around until it cooled enough to chew up and swallow.

'Yes, they're fresh out of the oven. Those are the mince pies I told you about.'

She'd disappeared straight after breakfast to the supermarket and came back triumphant with a jar of mincemeat, pre-made pie crusts and whipping cream.

'Your Aunt Eliza would make her own pastry, but I'm not that brave yet. We don't have any clotted cream either, so we'll have to make do.'

Clotted cream sounded unpleasant so he wasn't too sorry the local Kroger didn't stock the stuff. 'They're damn good.' Cole reached for another, but she smacked his hand away.

'There won't be enough for everyone to try if you scoff them all now.' Jenna checked her watch. 'I need to go and freshen up.

I'm sure your mum looks like an advert from one of those Christmas spreads in a glossy magazine.'

He rubbed a dab of flour off the end of her nose. 'The primping and fussing is to cover up the fact she's nervous. She's desperate for a miracle so we can buy back her shares, but deep down she's afraid it's too late.'

'Yes she is.'

Cole jerked around at the sound of his mother's weary voice. 'Sorry. I didn't mean—'

'To be overheard? But you're absolutely right.' She sleeked down her dress; the bright emerald colour struck him as harsh against her chalky skin. 'They'll be here soon, and I need to put the coffee on. Martin is back to his optimistic self and I'm trying to play along. This Christmas has been tough on him. All the invitations from our so-called friends have dried up. We haven't had any interest in the house yet and the mortgage is due again next week.'

He struggled to respond without lying outright.

'I'm sure viewing will pick up after the New Year. No one buys houses over Christmas.' Jenna's effort at a consoling comment earned her a slight shrug. 'You'll have to excuse me I need to hurry up and change into something more festive.'

'You look extremely pretty already, my dear. You always do.' His mother smiled. 'Someone not a million miles away loves you the way you are, and that's the most precious of gifts.'

'I know and I value it beyond anything.' Jenna squeezed Cole's hand as she walked by.

'Come on, Mom. Let's see to the coffee.' A pang of awareness struck him that this was how role-reversal looked. He was the one trying to take care of her instead of the other way around. Cole seized on the loud, jangling doorbell with relief.

The Landon family were never quiet when they gathered together and today was no exception. Jenna smiled at how determined everyone was to make their opinion heard. Yesterday's snow had turned to slush so the kids weren't interested in playing outside. With the teenagers tasked with taking care of the younger ones, they were engaged in an energetic game of hide and seek around the house. That only left Greg and Maggie's adorable new baby, Louisa, for the grown-ups to fuss over. Cole had laughed off his mother's concerns about what might get broken.

'As long as it's not a kid, it can be replaced. I've survived more than a few broken bones so that's not insurmountable either.'

The children had eaten more than their share of the sweet treats laid out in the dining room and now the adults had brought theirs around the fire while they chatted. Her mince pies were generally going down well, only Danny admitted he wasn't that keen but his wife, Cassie, ordered Jenna not to fret because he never touched anything made with dried fruit.

'You've made the house real pretty. It needed a woman's touch.' Eliza's praise made Jenna's face burn. 'It's lovely to see all your decorations, and I'm glad you kept the tree up for the kids to see today.'

'Why would we take it down?'

'Most folks do once Christmas is over.' Eliza nodded at her mother-in-law. 'Mimi had Adam get rid of ours this morning.'

'Our traditions are all different, I suppose,' Jenna mused. 'From what I've seen you decorate earlier than we usually do, but most English people keep their tree up until Twelfth Night on the sixth of January.'

'I'd be mighty tired of it by then,' Mimi scoffed. His grandmother never pulled any punches.

'Not everyone here is the same, Jenna,' Sylvia said. 'We always leave the decorations up at the distillery to help keep visitors in the festive spirit.'

'If you say so.' Mimi clearly wasn't convinced. 'Let's talk money before the kids come back.' She fixed her attention on Cole, and Jenna clasped his hand tighter. No matter how logical he understood this was, accepting help was still incredibly hard for him. 'How much are we talkin' about?'

'Two million.' His blunt statement made everyone's jaw drop. 'I can come up with maybe three hundred and fifty thousand and hopefully borrow a similar amount from the bank but that's it … unless I sell this place.'

'You're not doin' that, son.' Adam's forthright declaration stirred a chorus of agreement. 'I'd rather sell our house first.' He lost all his colour. 'If it wasn't for me, your daddy would still be here and this wouldn't be an issue.'

'Please tell me you aren't still blaming yourself for Trey's death?' Sylvia asked. 'If it was anyone's fault, it was mine.'

'How'd you figure that one out?' Cole asked.

'Because before he left to go hunting with you I told him … I was making plans to leave him.' Her eyes filled with tears. 'I'm sorry, sweetheart, but I was young and restless. Trey was a country boy at heart and I tried to change him.' She turned back to Adam. 'He was devastated because I said I was going to take Cole to live in South Carolina with me, where I grew up. My family were still there and I would've needed their help. I think if it was simply me leaving, poor Trey could've handled it, but he worshipped you and was a real hands-on father.'

'Mom, are you saying he deliberately—'

'No! He was distracted and angry so he got careless, that's all. I wouldn't have said anything now but I can't have Adam crucifying himself this way any longer. It's not fair.' She wrung her hands. 'That's my punishment to endure, not his.'

Jenna saw her push Martin's arm away when he tried to console her. 'We're supposed to be discussing how to buy my shares back, so let's concentrate on that.'

Jenna admired Sylvia's strength but her heart broke for Cole who looked as though he'd been slammed into a wall.

'We've talked it over,' Adam reached for his wife's hand, 'and our business is good so we're happy to invest in Landon Hollow. How does half a million sound?'

'Incredible, but you can't take that sort of risk.' Cole shook his head. 'I won't be responsible for you losing everything you've saved for your retirement and for the kids.' He waved around at his cousins. 'They'd never forgive me.'

'Hey pal, we'll speak for ourselves.' Danny put on his 'I'm-a-sheriff-don't-mess-with-me' voice. 'What Mom and Dad do with their money is their business. Cassie and I don't have that sort of money lying around, but we could come up with twenty thousand. Your business is rock solid. This was just an unfortunate situation.'

Jenna couldn't help noticing that no one looked directly at Martin. The conversation continued to bounce around, and the rest of Cole's cousins all offered to chip in. No one wanted to be the first to point out it still left Cole almost a million dollars short.

'I have something that might help. I'll be back in a minute.' Sylvia rose from her seat and disappeared towards their rooms at the back of the house. Nobody spoke until she returned, carrying a battered red leather case. 'This should cover most of the shortfall.' She placed it on the coffee table and opened the lid. 'The whole set is insured for three quarters of a million dollars.' Gasps fluttered around the room and everyone stared at the diamond and sapphire necklace with matching drop earrings and heavy bracelet glittering under the Christmas lights.

'My God, is that real?' Debbie's eyes stood out on ten-foot poles. She'd asked what they were all thinking.

Cole stared along with everyone else. The revelation that his parents' marriage had been falling apart when his father died was already too much to take in ... and now this? 'Where on earth did you get that from?'

'I didn't steal it, if that's what you're thinking.' His mother's attempt at a joke fell on stony ground. 'It's been in my family for generations and is always passed on to the oldest daughter.' Her face softened. 'I was saving it for your daughter one day.'

He felt sorry for Martin. This was humiliation on a grand scale. Knowing his wife could have saved them from financial ruin must have cut the man to the core. 'I can't possibly take it.' On so many levels, this was wrong.

'But you must.' Martin's quiet insistence bore no resemblance to his stepfather's usual pomposity. 'I'll never be able to live with myself if you don't.' He grasped his wife's hand. 'I don't blame you for keeping this quiet, my dear.' He pushed the jewellery case towards Cole. 'Take it. There's only one condition.' The flicker of a smile dragged at his grey face. 'I ... or rather, we ... want to be there when you break the good news to Ralph Bennett.'

'Sure.'

'I think we need to celebrate and drink a toast. You know what with.' Jenna's eyes glittered as brightly as the necklace.

'Remind me to tell you later how much I love you,' he whispered. Cole couldn't resist a quick kiss.

'Watch yourselves, the kids are comin' back.' Danny's warning came with a broad grin.

They poured out shots of Cornish Maid for the adults and spiced cider for the youngest Landons, then Cole clapped his hands. 'This is a special moonshine distilled specially for my lovely lady and its name is a nod to her heritage. Y'all know what she means to me already ... the last month has had some of the biggest ups and downs of my life, but I've got through it all with her.'

'He's conveniently forgetting, or being too polite to mention, that I caused a huge chunk of his troubles.' The colour bloomed in her cheeks. 'But I hope to make up for it over time.'

They passed the drinks around and everyone raised their glasses.

'To our great grandfathers and the best damn moonshine in the state of Tennessee.'

Chapter Twenty-Five

Jenna honed in on Cole's nerves when he kept reaching up to tug his baseball cap down tighter before remembering he wasn't wearing one. They were waiting in his office for Ralph Bennett to arrive, ostensibly to sort out the details of the man's involvement in Landon Hollow.

The week since Christmas had flown by, despite the distillery being as quiet as he predicted. Very few people were interested in taking the tours and the gift shop revenue had plummeted. When they had re-opened, Cole gathered all the staff together and told them plainly where things stood.

'I'm sorry I didn't tell y'all before, but I didn't want to ruin the holidays. My family have helped me to come up with a workable solution, but we won't find out for certain until next week if we've managed to pull off a rescue.'

That morning there was a sense of unease around the distillery because the moment of truth had arrived. On New Year's Eve, Jenna had turned down Cole's offer to drive into Nashville for the big fireworks display and concert in favour of staying home. Sylvia and Martin tactfully went to bed before midnight which left them to ring in the New Year alone, wrapped quietly in each other's arms in front of the fire.

'Should we take this down?' She pointed to the mistletoe still hanging over his desk. 'I don't want that creep getting the wrong idea.'

'No, leave it and come here.' He tugged her onto his lap and buried his face in her hair. 'You smell wonderful.'

'Is this when you liken me to a glass of Cornish Maid?'

Cole's eyes brightened. 'What's wrong with comparing you to the best tastin' shine to come out of Landon Hollow in a long while?'

'Absolutely nothing.'

'I thought y'all would be cryin' this morning.' Ralph swaggered in, all slicked back hair, tight black suit and smarmy expression today. 'Ready to talk business now, are you?' He sneered at Cole. 'Or are you too busy fraternising with the employees? Isn't that sexual harassment these days?'

She stood up and rested her hand on Cole's shoulder, praying he wouldn't overreact. 'Would you care for a coffee, Mr Bennett?'

'Sure. But call me Ralph, seein' as we're gonna be working together.'

'I don't think so.'

'Are you being unfriendly or quitting? I hope it's neither.'

Jenna ignored him and saw to their drinks. She placed two mugs in front of the men, set hers down next to Cole and then placed the two extra coffees she'd made by Ralph's right elbow.

'You expectin' us to drink a lot, sweetheart?'

A smile inched across Cole's face. 'Someone else wanted in on this meeting.'

'Is one of them your bank manager maybe?' Ralph scoffed. 'Bringing you a bag with two million dollars in hard cash, are they?'

She'd done her part with the drinks and had one more task. Jenna discreetly sent a text message. It was out of her hands now.

Cole's nerves were already in shreds before he spotted Sylvia and Martin approaching the door. 'Come in.' His yell startled Ralph Bennett who half-jumped out of the chair. 'I think y'all know each other.'

'I'm surprised you'd dare to show your faces.' Ralph glowered. 'I thought the boy wouldn't be speakin' to you by now.'

‘We’re family, Bennett.’ Martin clutched his wife’s hand and encompassed Cole with his tight smile. ‘That’s what you forgot. The Landons have all rallied around to remedy my mistake.’

Cole pushed a cheque across the table. ‘This is for the full amount, but you only get to keep this when I receive a legal document selling back my mother’s shares to me.’

‘That’s all very well, but I might’ve changed my mind.’ Ralph picked at his fingernails. ‘I reckon the price just went up.’

Jenna gave him a nod to remind him of the script they’d agreed to follow.

‘I don’t think so.’ He cleared his throat, set his phone on the desk and tapped the screen. The sound of Cole and Bennett’s voices came through clear as day, replaying the conversation they had before Christmas about Sylvia’s distillery shares.

‘Let’s get down to brass tacks how much do you want for my mother’s shares?’

‘They’re not for sale.’

‘How much?’

‘Two million.’

‘You’re fuckin’ kidding me.’

‘I don’t joke about business. If you want it badly enough you’ll find the money. If you don’t manage it, then I guess we’re gonna be partners come January.’

Cole stopped the recording and grinned. ‘We managed it, so let’s get this sorted.’

‘That won’t stand up in court,’ Bennett blustered.

‘Try it.’ He sat back, folded his arms and waited.

‘What I don’t get is why you’re goin’ along with this?’ Bennett snapped at Martin. ‘The money you got for the shares wasn’t enough to clear your debts so you’re still up to your ears in it unless the family is bailin’ you out too, and I kind of doubt that.’

‘Not that it’s any of your business, but we’re selling our house and a small rental property we own in Franklin. It’ll clear a large chunk of the money we owe and we've renegotiated the rest to pay back over time.' His stepfather's gaze rested on Cole. 'We're lucky that this fine young man is willing to share his home with us until we get straight again.'

'Rather you than me.' Bennett turned his sneering face back to Cole. 'Fine. Have your damn shares back. They aren't worth half what you're payin' for them.'

As far as Cole was concerned, they were priceless. 'My lawyer will contact yours later today. You can see yourself out.' He held his breath until his adversary stalked out and slammed the door behind him. '*Whew*. I wasn't sure we'd pull that off.'

'I was.' Jenna's confidence awed him, although it shouldn't have.

Martin covered his face with his hands and his mother broke into quiet sobs.

'Don't worry, these are happy tears,' Sylvia insisted, wiping ineffectually at her red-rimmed eyes and spreading mascara everywhere. 'It would've broken my heart if you'd lost control of the distillery because of … us.' She brushed off Martin's insistence that it was all down to him. 'I'm a grown woman and I should've paid attention when you tried to warn me about our finances. From now on, we're partners in everything.'

'Don't take what I'm gonna say the wrong way,' Cole spoke up, 'I'm damn pleased we've bought the shares back but if we hadn't succeeded, I'd still be a lucky man.' He pulled Jenna closer. 'I'm lucky because I've got the best family on the planet – and that includes you, Martin.' His stepfather's face crumpled. 'This amazing woman loves me, crazy though that seems some days. I'm passionate about my job and spend my days with the best co-workers a man could ask for.' He swallowed hard. 'None of us felt much like celebrating on New Year's Eve, so I'm declaring today the official Landon Hollow Distillery New Year. Tonight we're gonna throw the best damn party ever seen in Williamson County.'

Jenna slipped away from the noisy crowd for a few moments and wandered towards the back of the distillery. It hadn't been easy to throw together a party at short notice but between her, Sylvia, Eliza and Debbie, they'd pulled it off. She smoothed her hand over Bubbling Bertha and admired the gleaming copper still. Footsteps echoed on the concrete floor, and she turned to see Cole striding towards her.

'I missed you.' He slipped his strong, warm arms around her and rested his head against hers.

'Missed you too.' His distillery shirt retained the scent she'd grown to love; no matter how well they were washed, the lingering smell from the distillery never quite went away.

'I see Bertha is a rival for my affections. Should I be worried that you've fallen for her, too?'

Jenna laughed. 'She's definitely the third wheel in our relationship, but I'm okay with that if you are. More than okay.'

'You're a generous woman to share me that way.' He dragged a hot, heavy kiss over her mouth. 'Do you sometimes picture our great grandfathers standing next to each other out there in Moonshine Hollow passing a bottle of Lightning Flash back and forth between them? I imagine them hearing a twig snap and panicking that the revenuers have tracked them down, then breathing a sigh of relief when it turns out to be only a deer.'

'Yes, yes I do,' she whispered. 'And now a hundred years later, you're carrying on the tradition they started.'

'Oh, sweetheart. I understand it's too soon,' his voice cracked, 'so all I'm gonna say is that I hope we'll continue their legacy together … one day.'

'We will.' Jenna's promise made his eyes gleam. 'I've got to go back to England by mid-February because of my visa. Ninety days is the most I can stay at one visit. In case you're interested, Cornwall in springtime is hard to beat.' She let the thought hang for a moment. 'If that worked for you, we could come back here together afterwards.' *Was she assuming too much?*

'That all sounds near perfect to me.' His drawl thickened. 'We'll get things even closer to perfect when the time's right.'

'But what about the distillery? It won't run itself if you disappear over the pond.'

Cole's deep laugh rumbled through her. 'Tommy could run the production side with his eyes closed, and Debbie and Ashley are on top of the tours and retail. Y'all do have the internet in Cornwall I assume – and phones?'

'No, we're still using carrier pigeons and living in caves.' Jenna poked his ribs. 'The internet might be dodgy in a few remote places, but no more so than here.'

'Problem solved then.' He glanced back over his shoulder. 'I guess we should get back to the party. It's time to drink a toast to the future of Landon Hollow and to us. Before the Christmas decorations get taken down in a couple of days, I want to put this to good use again.' Cole whipped out a sprig of mistletoe and held it over Jenna's head. 'I'm gettin' quite a liking for this stuff.'

'You're not the only one.' She met his kiss half way. 'Mistletoe and moonshine make a pretty good combination if you ask me. Like us.'

* The End *

Thank You

I'm grateful to the lovely members of the Tasting Panel who fell in love with the idea of a moonshine-laced Christmas in Tennessee and, as always, to everyone who chooses to read my books. If you enjoy Jenna and Cole's story and have a minute to leave a review on Amazon, Goodreads or the site where you bought the book, I'd love to discover them filling up my Christmas stocking!

Angela

x

About the Author

Angela was born in St. Stephen, Cornwall, England. After completing her A-Levels she worked as a Naval Secretary. She met her husband, a US Naval Flight Officer while being based at a small NATO Headquarters on the Jutland Peninsula in Denmark. They lived together in Denmark, Sicily, California, southern Maryland and London before settling in Tennessee.

Angela took a creative writing course in 2000 and loved it so much that she has barely put her pen down since. She has had short stories and novels published in the US. Her debut novel, *Sugar & Spice*, won Choc Lit's Search for an American Star competition and is her UK debut.

Follow Angela:
Twitter: www.twitter.com/AngelaBritnell
Facebook: www.facebook.com/angelabritnell

More Choc Lit
from
Angela Britnell

Sugar and Spice

The Way to a Hero's Heart ...

Fiery, workaholic Lily Redman is sure of two things: that she knows good food and that she always gets what she wants. And what she wants more than anything is to make a success of her new American TV show, Celebrity Chef Swap – without the help of her cheating ex-fiancé and producer, Patrick O'Brien. So when she arrives in Cornwall, she's determined to do just that.

Kenan Rowse is definitely not looking for love. Back from a military stint in Afghanistan and recovering from a messy divorce and an even messier past, the last thing he needs is another complication. So when he lands a temporary job as Luscious Lily's driver, he's none too pleased to find that they can't keep their hands off each other!

But trudging around Cornish farms, knee deep in mud, and meetings with egotistical chefs was never going to be the perfect recipe for love – was it? And Lily could never fall for a man so disinterested in food – could she?

Visit www.choc-lit.com for more details

What Happens in Nashville

'What happens in Nashville, stays in Nashville!'
Claire Buchan is hardly over the moon about the prospect of her sister's hen party; travelling from the UK to Nashville, Tennessee, for a week of honky-tonks, karaoke and cowboys. Certainly not straight-laced Claire's idea of a good time, what with her lawyer job and sensible boyfriend, Philip.

But then she doesn't bank on meeting Rafe Castello. On the surface, Rafe fits the cowboy stereotype with his handsome looks and roguish charm but as he and Claire get to know each other, she realises there is far more to him than meets the eye.

Can Claire keep to the holiday mantra of 'what happens in Nashville, stays in Nashville' or will she find that some things are far too difficult to simply leave behind?

Visit www.choc-lit.com for more details

Celtic Love Knot

Can two tangled lives make a love knot?
Lanyon Tremayne is the outcast of his small Cornish village of St. Agnes. Susceptible to fits of temper and with a chequered past behind him, he could even be described as a bit of an ogre. But nobody knows the painful secret he hides.

Olivia Harding has learnt a thing or two about ogres. She's a professor from Tennessee, specialising in Celtic mythology and has come to St. Agnes to research the legend of a Cornish giant – and to lay to rest a couple of painful secrets of her own.

But when Olivia meets the ruggedly handsome Lanyon, her trip to Cornwall looks set to become even more interesting. Will she get through to the man beneath the bad-tempered façade, or is Lanyon fated to be the 'ogre' of St. Agnes forever?

Visit www.choc-lit.com for more details

The Wedding Reject Table

Once on the reject table, always on the reject table?
When Maggie Taylor, a cake decorator, and Chad Robertson, a lawyer from Nashville Tennessee, meet at a wedding in Cornwall it's not under the best circumstances. They have both been assigned to 'the reject table', alongside a toxic collection of grumpy great aunts, bitter divorcees and stuffy organists.

Maggie has grown used to being the reject, although when Chad helps her out of a wedding cake disaster she begins to wonder whether the future could hold more for her. But will Chad be strong enough to deal with the other problems in Maggie's life? Because a ruined cake isn't the only issue she has – not by a long shot.

Here Comes the Best Man

Being the best man is a lot to live up to …
When troubled army veteran and musician Josh Robertson returns home to Nashville to be the best man at his younger brother Chad's wedding he's just sure that he's going to mess it all up somehow.

But when it becomes clear that the wedding might not be going to plan, it's up to Josh and fellow guest Louise Giles to make sure that Chad and his wife-to-be Maggie get their perfect day.

Can Josh be the best man his brother needs? And is there somebody else who is beginning to realise that Josh could be her 'best man' too?

Visit www.choc-lit.com for more details

Love Me for a Reason

Love doesn't always have to make sense …
When Daisy Penvean meets Nathaniel Dalton whilst visiting a friend in Nashville, it seems there are a million and one reasons for them not to be together. Nathaniel's job as a mergers and acquisitions manager means sharp suits and immaculate hair, whereas Daisy's work as a children's book illustrator lends itself to a more carefree, laidback style. And, as Daisy lives in England, there's also the small matter of the Atlantic Ocean between them.

But when Nathaniel's job takes him to London to oversee the merger of a small publisher with a large American company, he and Daisy meet again under very different circumstances. Because Daisy works for the publisher involved in the deal, and if Nathaniel does his job, it could mean she loses hers …

Visit www.choc-lit.com for more details

You're the One that I Want

What if you didn't want to fake it any more?
When Sarah, a teacher from Cornwall, and Matt, a businessman from Nashville, meet on a European coach tour, they soon find themselves in a relationship … Except it's a fake relationship. Because Matt is too busy for romance, and Sarah is only trying to make her cheating ex-husband jealous … isn't she?

As Matt and Sarah complete their tour of Europe, they do all the things real couples are supposed to do – from visiting fairy-tale castles in Germany to recreating the scene from Romeo and Juliet in Verona. And, of course, for every picturesque destination there's a loved-up selfie and Facebook post to match.

But as their holiday comes to an end, Sarah and Matt realise that they're not happy with their pretend relationship. They want the real thing.

Visit www.choc-lit.com for more details

Christmas at Black Cherry Retreat

What if you had nowhere to call home for Christmas?
When Fee Winter books a winter break at the remote Black Cherry Retreat in the small town of Pine Ridge, Tennessee, it's with the idea that the peace and quiet will help her recuperate from her hectic life as a photographer.

But what she didn't bank on was meeting Tom Chambers and his huge, interfering yet lovable family. With them, could Fee finally experience the warmth and support that's been missing from her own life – and maybe even find a place to call home in time for Christmas?

Visit www.choc-lit.com for more details

One Summer in Little Penhaven

Could one summer change your life?

When high-flying American lawyer Samantha Muir finds out she's lost her partnership whilst on an assignment in London, she has a dramatic reaction.

Rather than returning home, she resigns, leaves her business suits behind and jumps on the first train to Cornwall at the encouragement of a friendly stranger.

The village of Little Penhaven, where Samantha eventually ends up, is a world away from her life in Knoxville, Tennessee – and local farmer Cadan Day is certainly a world away from any man she has met before. But could the Cornish village and Cadan play a part in Samantha's summer of self-discovery?

Visit www.choc-lit.com for more details

Christmas in Little Penhaven

Have yourself a little Cornish Christmas ...

Wannabe author Jane Solomon is expecting an uneventful Christmas in her Cornish village of Little Penhaven. But then super fit American gym owner Hal Muir comes to town, and suddenly the holiday season looks set to be far more interesting. Hal is keen on embracing every British tradition on offer, from mince pies to Christmas pub quizzes – and perhaps some festive romance too ...

Visit www.choc-lit.com for more details

New Year, New Guy

Out with the old life, in with the new …

When Laura's bride-to-be sister, Polly, organises a surprise reunion for her fiancé and his long lost American friend, Laura grudgingly agrees to help keep the secret. And when the plain-spoken, larger-than-life Hunter McQueen steps off the bus in her rainy Devon town and only just squeezes into her tiny car, it confirms that Laura has made a big mistake in going along with her sister's crazy plan.

But could the tall, handsome man with the Nashville drawl be just what reserved Laura Williams needs to shake up her life and start something new?

Visit www.choc-lit.com for more details

A Summer to Remember in Herring Bay

Essy Havers is good at finding things. Her company specialises in helping clients track down anything, from missing china pieces to rare vintage clothing. But now Essy has something more important to find: herself.

Essy has always been curious about her mother's secret past and her Cornish roots. So, when the opportunity arises, she hops on a plane in Tennessee and ends up in Herring Bay in Cornwall; the village where her mother grew up.

But once there, she's mystified by the reactions of the villagers when they realise who she is. Was Essy's decision to visit Cornwall a mistake, or will it lead to a summer she'll never forget?

Visit www.choc-lit.com for more details

Introducing Choc Lit

We are an independent publisher creating a delicious selection of fiction.
Where heroes are like chocolate – irresistible!
Quality stories with a romance at the heart.

See our selection here: **www.choc-lit.com**
We would love to hear how you enjoyed *Christmas at Moonshine Hollow*. Please leave a review on the retail site where you purchased this novel or visit **www.choc-lit.com** and give your feedback.

Choc Lit novels are selected by genuine readers like yourself. We only publish stories our Tasting Panel want to see in print. Our reviews and awards speak for themselves.

Could you be a Star Selector and join our Tasting Panel?
Would you like to play a role in choosing which novels we decide to publish? Do you enjoy reading women's fiction? Then you could be perfect for our Tasting Panel.
Visit here for more details:
www.choc-lit.com/join-the-choc-lit-tasting-panel

Keep in touch:
Sign up for our newsletter for all the latest news and offers:
www.spread.choc-lit.com.

Follow us on Twitter: @ChocLituk
and Facebook: Choc Lit

Printed in Great Britain
by Amazon

87051163R00112